LOVE, SIVVY

A Novel Inspired by the
Life, Letters, and Diaries
of Young Sylvia Plath

R. L. Toalson

LITTLE, BROWN AND COMPANY
LARGE PRINT EDITION

Content Warning
This book contains references to clinical depression, suicidal ideation, and suicide.

In order to give a sense of time and place, some names of real people, places, or events have been included in the book; however, the content of this book is the product of the author's imagination.

Copyright © 2026 by R. L. Toalson

Ornamental decor copyright © by A-R-T/Shutterstock.com

Cover art copyright © 2026 by Kimberly Glyder. Cover design by Gabrielle Chang. Cover copyright © 2026 by Hachette Book Group, Inc.
Interior design by Carla Weise.

Hachette Book Group supports the right to free expression and the value of copyright. The purpose of copyright is to encourage writers and artists to produce the creative works that enrich our culture.

The scanning, uploading, and distribution of this book without permission is a theft of the author's intellectual property. If you would like permission to use material from the book (other than for review purposes), please contact permissions@hbgusa.com. Thank you for your support of the author's rights.

Little, Brown and Company
Hachette Book Group
1290 Avenue of the Americas, New York, NY 10104
Visit us at LBYR.com

First Edition: February 2026

Little, Brown and Company is a division of Hachette Book Group, Inc. The Little, Brown name and logo are registered trademarks of Hachette Book Group, Inc.

The publisher is not responsible for websites (or their content) that are not owned by the publisher.

Little, Brown and Company books may be purchased in bulk for business, educational, or promotional use. For information, please contact your local bookseller or the Hachette Book Group Special Markets Department at special.markets@hbgusa.com.

Library of Congress Cataloging-in-Publication Data

Names: Toalson, R. L. (Rachel L.) author
Title: Love, Sivvy : a novel inspired by the life, letters, and diaries of young Sylvia Plath / R.L. Toalson.
Description: First edition. | New York : Little, Brown and Company, 2026. | Includes bibliographical references. | Audience: Ages 14 and Up | Summary: A novel-in-verse follows Sylvia Plath through her high school and college years as she struggles between societal expectations, mental health challenges, and her fierce ambition to become a poet.
Identifiers: LCCN 2025013026 | ISBN 9780316587136 hardcover | ISBN 9780316587143 ebook
Subjects: CYAC: Plath, Sylvia—Fiction | Novels in verse | Depression, Mental—Fiction | Sex role—Fiction | Self-actualization—Fiction | LCGFT: Novels in verse | Biographical fiction
Classification: LCC PZ5.T4578 Lo 2026
LC record available at https://lccn.loc.gov/2025013026

ISBNs: 978-0-316-58713-6 (hardcover), 978-0-316-58714-3 (ebook), 978-0-316-61047-6 (large print)

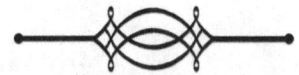

For Julie Jimerson,
who challenged me to
read the greats
and write my own
masterpieces

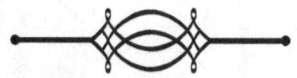

*I am a genius of a writer;
I have it in me. I am writing the best poems
of my life; they will make my name.*
—SYLVIA PLATH, 1962

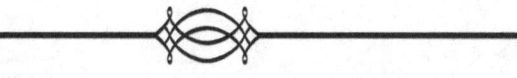

Born to Be Remembered

Junior Year, 1948–1949

1

I was born to be remembered.

That's not the sort of thing
you can tell other people
or even say out loud,

> especially when you have
> the wrong anatomy.

But it's the kind of thing
you know
deep down inside.

2

I watch my fellow students
stream through the doors
of Bradford Senior High.

Girls giggle,
link arms, smile at the boys
glancing their way.
The boys could care less.

It's all so ridiculous.
Yet I smile at the boys, too.
Just because you have
grand goals for your future
doesn't mean you can't
fall in love.

I follow the crowd into the halls,
one tiny fish in a
gigantic ocean.

But by the time I'm done with
Bradford Senior High,

    I'll stand out.
            I know I will.

3

My best subject is English.

Virginia Woolf,
Dylan Thomas,
Wallace Stevens,
I devour them.

When I speak up,
everyone quiets.
Like they know
I have something important
to say.

4

Mr. Crockett is my favorite teacher.
He's brilliant and passionate
and recognizes the difference
between fluff and important literature.

There are only fifteen of us
in his advanced seminar.
We call ourselves the Crocketteers.

I leave his class believing
that my dreams
               are within reach.

I've never written
so much about
Hardy, Joyce, Auden,
Woolf, Dylan Thomas,
Shakespeare, and Milton.

I write literary criticism
and by the time I've finished,
two poems have also
scribbled themselves
onto a page.

5

Ruth, Margot, and Betsy
enjoy their studies,
but I'm not sure they enjoy them
half as much as I do.

Between classes they talk about boys.
Robert, William, Richard, Gary.
He's so cute,
he's really nice,
his hand brushed against mine…

it's like their happiness is tied to

whether or not a boy
looks at them.

"Are you going to the dance?" Betsy says.

"The dance?" I raise an eyebrow,
as though I don't know about the dance.
It's been on my calendar
since the day they announced it.

"You know," she says.
"It's only the biggest social event
of the year."

Dances don't matter, I remind myself.

It's complicated living
in the kind of world where
the worst thing
you can do for your ambitious future

      is fall in love.

6

If poetry were a boy,

I would marry him.
I would cook for him,
clean for him,
give him a hundred children—
more, even—
deliver him words
shaped into song.

Then no one could say,
"But, Sylvia, don't you want to
marry and have children?"

"But, Sylvia, don't you know
you can't be a good wife and mother
if you also have a career?"

"But, Sylvia, don't you know what
being a woman means?"

7

This year I'm determined
not to let school get the best of me,
not to put so much pressure on myself
    to make the perfect grades,

not to let my high expectations send me
    into a pit of self-criticism
as they've done in the past.

I have new goals:

    enjoy my life while I'm young
    don't let school become a prison
    rest when I need it (rather than
        waiting until I'm sick).

I will read
I will write
I will dream.

(And maybe:
I will fall in love.)

8

Mother peers inside our room.
"How was school, Sivvy?"

I'm listing my new goals in a notebook.
I nod toward the page, tell her,

"Well, Mother, this year
I will not let anxiety
rule my studies."

She looks at me like
she doesn't quite believe me.

I glare at her,
but I can't blame her.
She knows me too well.
Still, a mother should pretend
so her daughter believes
anything is possible.
Shouldn't she?

The problem is,
I want to be the best.
And how do you become the best?

You chase perfection.

I've chased it since
I was old enough to
write a verse.

9

My mood today swings
between black and yellow,
a tempest.

Who knows what brought
this on. That's the
most disturbing piece of the

   high, low, high, low, high, low.

Maybe it was my B mark in science,
maybe it was anticipating rejection
for the poems I sent to *Seventeen*,
maybe it was simply a little gloomy
and gray today.

If I could predict my ricochets,
I would have more control.

Mother checks on me far too often.
She hovers just outside our bedroom.
I want to shout at her to go to Warren.
He may still need her, but I don't.

I'm nearly an adult.
She can't hover forever.

My head aches.
I press my face into my pillow.

I haven't slept well since
I mailed that envelope to *Seventeen*.

I need to get back to
     reading,
   studying,
go out for a walk,
     eat better.

For now, I just want to
curl up and close my eyes.

Mother slips into my room,
sits on my bed,
strokes my head
until
I
fall
asleep.

10

Boys can talk
all they want about
   necking, kissing, touching,

but a young lady can't express
the barest hint of desire
to do any of those things.

It's not proper for a young lady
to even think about such improper acts.

It's not proper for a young lady
to imagine what she would do
if a boy took her driving one evening,
    parked,
  wrapped his arms around her,
and kissed her in a way she'd
never been kissed before.

And it's certainly not proper for a young lady
to ache for those experiences

    so desperately

she feels she might burn from
the inside out.

I'm exhausted with being
a proper young lady.

11

A poem, accepted!
Is there anything
better than
receiving the news
that your work will appear
in a publication
thousands of people
will read?

Is there anything
more terrifying?

12

Today in seminar Mr. Crockett
congratulated me on my future publication.
Someone in the back of the room

coughed around the word "Fluff."
I know exactly who it was.
                    Peter.
I don't even know
why he's in this class—
probably because his dad's
the superintendent of the school.

Peter doesn't think girls
should be allowed
in a college-level class.
He's never said so
in front of Mr. Crockett,
but he's made it explicitly clear
outside of class.

Mr. Crockett keeps me a little late.
"I'd like to see some of your
short stories published before
you leave Bradford," he tells me.

Peter waits outside the class,
pretending to fix
a paper poster on the wall.
I pass him without a word,
but he follows,

a detached shadow
stretching long and mean.

"You know you'll never
go anywhere," he says.

"We'll see about that," I say.

"It's pity publishing," he says.
"For a fluff magazine.
Nothing more.
It doesn't mean anything."

Why do his words
sound so much like
the voice in my head?

"One day you'll have to choose," he says.
"Marriage or career.
And if you choose wrong,
you'll spend the rest of your life

    alone."

13

I know what the world

thinks about
    women like me.

I try not to care.
The truth is, I want it all.
Marriage *and* a career.

14

I can't write the poem
I want to write.
My mind feels blank.

I have lived
such a small existence.
I long to see the African savanna,
the lights of Paris,
the beauty of the English moors
the Brontës brought to life.

How do you write
anything that matters
if you've never experienced
anything that matters?

My pen
struggles to make sense of

Daddy's death,
describes the weather
outside my window,
and the barely there leaves
of the oak
reinvigorated
after a cold winter.

I scratch out
every word I write
and throw my notebook
across the room.
It slides under my dresser.

Good riddance.

15

Mother asks me how I'm doing.

     The truth is,
I'm a bit overwhelmed,
a snake pit has swallowed me,
and I can't see
how to climb back out.
But I smile and say,

"Everything is wonderful."

I know how to play the part.

16

I can't get anything
less than an A,
since college applications
will be due next year and
I know Mother doesn't
have the money to pay
for higher education.

She has enough to worry about.
She had to borrow money
from Grammy and Grampy again.
Grampy is too old to work,
but he'll never slow down.
He has too many people to support.

I don't want to be another.

Sometimes I imagine
that if Daddy were here,
everything would be easier.

We'd have more money.
Mother wouldn't have to work so hard.
Maybe Warren and I could
go to college without
running ourselves ragged trying to
    make the best grades,
      get the best scholarships,
        prove we belong in higher education.

Do I only miss him because
he'd make things easier?
Is he a story I tell myself I need?

After dinner
I close my door and
work on my analysis of T. S. Eliot
for Mr. Crockett's class and
try to produce nothing short of

        perfection

because I do have to
    make the best grades and
    get the best scholarships
if I want a future.

Every word I write is rubbish.

17

I'm named coeditor of *The Bradford*,
the high school newspaper,
along with Frank Irish.

The column that announces
my new position refers to my
   "exceptional ability as a writer,"
   "noteworthy reputation of sticking
     to a task until it's done,"
   and "keen critical eye."

Maybe not *every* word I write is rubbish.

Work, Date, Write, Repeat

Summer 1949

1

Junior year finished,
just like that.
With excellent marks.

And now it's summer.

This one,
   I tell myself,
will be different.

For one thing,
I will date every boy
who asks me out.

I will burn and kiss and
neck and do whatever I want.
No attachments.

Maybe I will be too forward,

maybe I will not appear prim enough,
maybe I will be
        too much too much too much

but I will not be swayed by
society's definitions of
who I must be
because I'm a woman.
And I will not settle
for less than I,
        Sylvia,
want.

Why would I make myself
miserable for
someone else's benefit?
Too many women
do that every day.

I will not be one of them.

2

John Hodges
goes to Denison University,
and he's just about flawless:

tall
athletic
gorgeous.

We play tennis
on the Wellesley College courts.
He takes me on soda dates
and drives me around.

Our time alone makes me nervous,
but I pretend it doesn't.

I'm weary of pretending.
It's what you do, isn't it?
As a woman.
Pretend you're happy.
Pretend you're capable.
Pretend you're completely content
with the tiny little sliver of life
they permit you to have.

But I can't hold it
against John, can I?
Most men are simply...
        oblivious.

3

Bruce Ellwell takes me to
some car races in Westboro.
I don't expect to enjoy it,
but I do.

    The roar of engines,
        the exciting accidents,
    the collisions and destruction.

Am I heartless?

After it's over I want to go
parking with Bruce,
which seems wrong
after what we've watched.

Passion is confusing.

4

I work, date, write, repeat.

I love the summer,
    the lack of pressure,

>   the sea breeze,
> the sun bronzing my skin.

I love long walks along the beach
on the arm of a handsome godlike boy.
I run through them like experiments.
None of them last long.
I'm not sure if it's me or them.

I let them kiss me,
>   embrace me,
but something stops me
from doing more.

Does my desire scare me?
Do I *want* more?

I know I want to be desired
because I am Sylvia Plath,
not because I'm a woman
in a pretty dress.

I am afraid, though.
I'm afraid of appearing
>   too forward,
> too loose.
I'm afraid of everyone

calling me a tease,
saying I'm cheap.
Girls are supposed to have
pristine reputations.

It seems that no matter
how you examine the world—
     work, desire, passion, living—
it all circles back to this:

A woman is kept in place
by a host of rules
she'll never fully understand.

Young ladies can never be

     free.

5

Betsy and I used to swoon over
Greg Hall at Wellesley basketball games.
He was so far from the realm
of possible boyfriends then.
It's a dream come true that
I'm dating him now!
How lucky can a girl get?

"I love you," he says,
but he doesn't pressure me to
give him more than
I'm willing to give.
He says sex is one of the
loveliest acts in the world.
He doesn't want to
cheapen it with pressure.

He gives me space,
and he tells me exactly
how he feels about me.

Does a more marvelous boy exist?

Twenty-one boys
since my junior year—
I had to go through them all
to find Greg Hall.

6

I spend every day
with Greg.
We play tennis.
We take long walks

in the woods and
around the lake and
look at stars.

Today we drive to Cape Cod
with friends.
It's as close to bliss
as I can expect in this life.

We lie on striped towels,
the sea whispering secrets,
and every salty breath
feels like a gift.

I enjoy my life alone,
but enjoying life with
someone like Greg
is an electric thrill.

        Is this love?

7

Before Greg leaves
for Williams College
we exchange photos.
No promises,
which is fine by me.

I keep his photo in
my journal.

8

The end of summer
sends my moods
   up down
   up down
   sideways

completely unpredictable

Everything sets me off—
Mother coming to my room
asking questions most mothers ask—

   How was your day?
   What have you written?
   Another date tonight?

Warren chattering endlessly
at dinner about
nothing of consequence,
just a collection of
meaningless words about
meaningless things

>   (How nice it would be
>   to be a confident man
>   instead of a woman
>   so full of self-doubt
>   she would sink in the Dead Sea)

My moods are
   up down
   up down
   sideways

completely unpredictable

And everyone is
getting weary of me

        Especially myself

9

Greg's not the one for me.
That becomes clear in
how little I miss him
while he's gone.

Maybe it's for the best
that I don't find

my ideal man in
my entire summer of dating.

It stands to reason that
a woman who
doesn't *really* know
what she wants
won't find
what she wants.

Maybe it's for the best
that I don't become
like so many others:
engaged at seventeen,
married at eighteen.

Maybe it's for the best
that the perfect man
remains a figment of
my imagination.

The World Awaits

Senior Year, 1949–1950

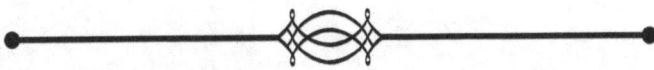

1

A room of my own—
    what magic is this?

Warren's gone to Exeter,
so Mother moves out of
the bedroom we've shared
for ages.

No more
   constant nagging.
No more
   asking if I'm getting out of bed.
No more
   hawk eye watching my every move.

No more trying to write
with another person
and her arduous expectations
         hovering.

How long has it been
since I had a room
of my own?

Too long.

I feel like I can breathe.

2

Senior year begins with
Mr. Crockett saying,
"Well, students, it's your
last year to participate
in this seminar.
What will you do?
Where will you go?"

I always have an answer
to this question.

I will
   publish more poems
      and short stories
   apply to college
      (finances be damned!)

stay focused, positive, and productive
so I accomplish these goals.

No more depression!
　No more ricocheting moods!
　　No more worry!

I will myself
　　　to fully live.

3

Mr. Crockett pulls me aside
after class. "Do you know where
you want to continue
your education, Miss Plath?" he says.

I don't remind him
there aren't many choices
for young women—
but at least the schools
we have are good ones.

"Wellesley or Smith," I say.

He nods. "Good schools."

What would it be like
to be a man,
to have infinite possibilities?

What would it be like
not to have to explain
why you don't want
to be a teacher
or just get married?

What would it be like
not to have to prove yourself
every
   step
      of
         the way?

I look at the floor
when I say,
"It depends
on money, though."

Mr. Crockett doesn't seem
the least bit bothered by this.
"Scholarships," he says.
"Probably several."

"You really think so?"

"In all my years,
I've never taught a student
so bright and talented," he says.

I wait for him to make
that qualification—
  for a girl.

But he doesn't.

He only says, "I'll write
your recommendation letters.
Tell me where,
and it's done."

Possibility swells in my chest.

Maybe I can
  dream and write
  and be myself
  and break the mold
  and become somebody great someday
 just like I always planned.

Maybe I can have it

        a l l.

4

My friends don't consider
money an obstacle.
Their parents set up
a college fund the day
they were born.
They have money enough
for tuition and housing
and don't have to base
their decision about
where they go to school
on how much scholarship money
they get
or how much babysitting money
they save.

I wonder if they know
how lucky they are.

My friends don't have to
    study study study
for school exams or

worry about SAT scores or
consider and reconsider
everything they say
on a college application or
volunteer for a thousand
different school committees
and the Girl Scouts
and the Unitarian youth group
to make themselves
look more appealing.
They can put in a
    good enough effort
and that's enough.

But I have to be
    excellent.
I have to finish a test
and go over the answers
again and again and again
to ensure everything is as right
as I know how to make it,
because one test could
stand between college and me.
    One screwup,
        one terrible essay,
      one missed line
on an application.

My friends go to school.
I go to school, work, volunteer,
   write, publish, repeat
because the world is not yet mine
like it is theirs.

Some days I remind myself
all this effort teaches me
     persistence
     a good work ethic
     how to chase a dream with
   everything I am.
Sometimes I rage that
this is my lot in life.

The difference between
     them and me
sometimes feels

     insurmountable.

5

What are the benefits of
going steady with a boy?
No one can tell me.

My friends are marrying young—
many right after high school.
Can you imagine?

Mother is ecstatic
every time a boy comes by.
She can't hide her hopes,
but I've realized I don't want to
be attached to one person right now.
I want to date around.
Meet as many young men as I can.
Keep things casual.

I know the world doesn't like
young women who date
more than one boy.
I don't care.

Maybe I don't want to love
    just one man.
Or maybe I don't want to love
    any.
Who's to say
   what's right for me
except me?

6

I'm drowning in
   college applications
   school exams
   SAT preparation—
but I finally get a short story accepted.
It'll be in the November *Seventeen*.

Because of my moods,
Mother's worried about
the psychological test
I need for Smith admissions.

I'm more worried about money.

Do I dare dream?

7

Sometimes I wonder
if dates are dangerous.

My body is a wild blaze.
I want more than kisses on
mouths and cheeks and necks.

I want to know every inch
of a man's body.
I want to feel the victory of
hearing my lover groan in pleasure.
I want to experience
the power of possession
moments before I surrender
to the heat that pulses inside.

Tonight Bob Riedeman takes me out.
He used to be a Crocketteer
and studies at the University of
New Hampshire now.
Tall, blue-eyed, blond,
so handsome I melt.

I kiss him and ache for more.
    But conventionality doesn't
allow it.
We tear ourselves
away from each other.

Does he feel me burn?

Does he burn for me?

8

Mother taps on my door.
"Sivvy? It's time for dinner."

All I seem to do anymore is
    stare into space
  sleep
    try to eat
  sleep
    do it all again.
I haven't written in days.

"Grammy and Grampy
are here," Mother says.
"They've brought early gifts."

We're celebrating Christmas today.
I didn't manage any
gifts this year, which
only makes me feel worse.
But still I follow Mother
out to the parlor.

The table is set with a feast.
Grammy and Grampy kiss me

and say how glad they are to see me.
No one mentions college
or writing or even the way
I push food around on my plate,
pick at potatoes,
eat a few string beans,
pop a handful of red grapes
and nearly gag.

After dinner we open gifts.
They got me a pretty sweater and a skirt,
one I'll probably save for graduation,
and a silver pen
with my name engraved on it.

"So you can write
more brilliant poems," Grampy says.

I don't know whether to
    laugh or cry.

9

Mother wants me to
live at college, even if

I choose Wellesley.
She says it's important for
the college experience.

She didn't get to live on campus.
I think this is her trying to
make up for something
she was denied.

The problem is money.

Smith's tuition is
eight hundred fifty dollars a year,
and room and board's
another seven hundred fifty—

    much more than Mother can pay!

She says she can contribute
four hundred dollars a year
if I decide to live at school,
but that's not enough.
I need a scholarship.
I absolutely must get one.

Pressure, pressure, pressure.

10

Mr. Crockett's taking
the Crocketteers to Europe
for a bicycle trip.

Well, he's taking
the ones who can afford it.
What would I give to go?
            Anything.

They'll see plays,
visit music festivals,
ride down the Rhine,
do all kinds of
        wonderful, magical, beautiful
things.

And I'll be here,
working, saving for college,
wishing upon a star.

Hoping one day
my luck and fortune
will change.

11

I'm getting lost in Sigrid Undset.
A woman who won
the Nobel Prize for Literature!
She's brilliant.
She clearly understands
what it means to be
a woman in love.
I read every book she's written.
The last three years we've studied
mostly men in literature.
It's refreshing to read fiction
by and about women.

I see myself,
and that makes me want to
      be myself.

12

I take tedious care
on my Smith application.
Everything must be flawless.
There's no room for error.

I list my extracurricular activities:

    viola
    orchestra
    piano
    The Bradford
    tennis
    basketball
    yearbook
    school devotional committee
    school decoration committee
    Girl Scouts
    Unitarian youth group
    United World Federalists

SAT verbal: 700
SAT math: 567

I list all my prizes for
    writing
    art
    academics

I mention the authors
who influence me:
        Amy Lowell

Robert Frost
T. S. Eliot
Edna St. Vincent Millay
Virginia Woolf
Shakespeare
Emerson
Tolstoy

The whole thing
feels like peacocking.
Look at me,
   hear me ring my bell,
      witness how spectacular I am.

I tell myself
men do it all the time.

        Why shouldn't I?

13

I peck away at
Mother's typewriter
for eight hours,
a full-time job.
I don't even break for lunch.

Mother hovers,
trying to convince me to eat,
but she's the one who told a friend,
> "She just has to get this scholarship.
> There's no other way."

If I want college,
it's up to me.

That's a heavy burden,
but I can handle heavy burdens,
so long as I

> work work work
> > write write write

and leave nothing to chance.

14

"Come take a break," Mother says.
"Can't," I say. "Too much to do."
"You're working too hard," Mother says.
"You know what happens when you work too hard."

It usually means dark days ahead.

And what kind of future do you have if
you're too weary to enjoy it?

Mother's almost disappeared
from the hallway by the time
I scramble up.

"What did you have in mind, Mother?"

Her smile lights
the whole world.

15

Mr. Crockett gives me
the most wonderful
recommendation letter.
He calls me the best student
he's ever taught.

Maybe it's just something
teachers say. But I'd like to think
he's telling the truth.

I include a recommendation letter
from my principal and Mrs. Aldrich,

who uses me for babysitting.

Everything in my application is ready.

Am I?

16

Mother flutters
in and out of my room,
like a butterfly startled into flight,
too busy to rest.

I'm sick.
She doesn't like it when
I'm sick.

She sets warm broth
on my bedside table,
along with a cup of water.

"Drink the broth first," she says.
"Then the water.
Both will flush out
whatever you've got."

I want to tell her that
whatever I've got
can't be so easily flushed out.
Can I live like this
for the rest of my life?
All this pressure.
All her expectations.
The awful weight of trying and failing.

Go away! I want to shout.
Leave me alone!
Don't you know
your hopes and dreams for me
make all this worse?
But I bite my tongue.

I remind myself
this darkness
   this ocean of despair
never lasts forever.

I turn over,
pull the covers over my head,
pretend to sleep
until long after the broth turns cold.

17

Perfect
perfect
perfect
perfect
perfect

When did I learn
the only thing
a woman could be
was perfect?

We're taught it from birth:
    stand up straight
  sit like a lady
think like a lady
  act like a lady
    smile
  stay quiet
don't take up too much space
  blend in

    and for god's sake
  stop all that silly thinking.

The world tells me I must be
           perfect
a perfect wife
   a perfect mother
      a perfect woman...

How do you attain perfection
when you are so far from

       perfect?

18

May already.
Graduation is right around
the corner. Am I ready?
I'd like to think I am.
There's a great big world
out there to explore,
and this will be
my opportunity.

At the same time...
What if I get lost in it?
What if my moods intensify?
What if I can't manage on my own?

Growing up happened so fast.
I couldn't wait to grow up
when I was a child and now,
    here I am,
        almost grown,
and I wish I could be a child again.

So few decisions.
Such small expectations.
So few opportunities for
        disappointment and ruin.

The last eighteen years
have sped by so fast,
how can I not assume
the next eighteen years
will do the same?

Before I'm ready,
before I can blink and decide
who I want to be,
before I'm finished with
all the masterpieces I must write,
I will be old and gray.

Time, you are the worst of all teases.
Slow, I say, and you speed.

Speed, I say, and you slow.
I cannot seem to master you.

19

The Bradford weighs on me.
I never have enough time
to make sure every issue is error-free.

Once it prints,
I never read it.
I don't want proof of
how imperfect it is.

But at least it keeps me busy.

Idle time leaves
too much space for
morbid thoughts.

20

The acceptance letter comes.

Wellesley College! And a scholarship!

What about Smith, my first choice?
Am I okay living a second-choice life?

It's better than nothing.
I try to make that enough.

21

I keep submitting
my poetry and short stories.
A magazine here,
a magazine there.

Mother mails the submissions for me.

"She sees herself in you,
you know," Warren says.
"You're living her dream."
It's true that Mother wanted to write.
She was an English teacher
before Daddy asked her
to become a homemaker instead.
She wrote some pieces
of his scientific papers.
And then he died and left her
with two kids to raise.

She had to take what jobs she could.

Sometimes I think Warren's right.
She's trying to live
through me.

Does she understand
how heavy her hopes are?

22

Every time Mother checks the mail
I rush to see news. But there is
     nothing nothing nothing.

I guess the choice is made.
At least I get to continue my studies.

And Wellesley *is* a good school.

But it's also a school
trapped in time.

A place where women learn
how to be good wives and mothers,
taking with them enough education

to hold a riveting dinner conversation
with guests.
Hardly a place where
women go to learn
all there is to know
about everything.

Perhaps Smith
would have been the same.

This I do know:
I will not let Wellesley's
conventional culture
smother me,
    bind me smaller,
        misshape me.
I will tear down the cage,
    storm through the rubble,
    unfold my wings.

Did you forget
that I was born for
        greatness?

I refuse to live
a boxed-in life.

23

Maybe Wellesley is a gift
from the universe,
not something that will keep me small
but something that will explode me into

>   Sylvia Plath,
>   the woman who will be remembered.

But I won't have freedom.
Wellesley is so close to home that
Mother will know everything—
    every date
    every meal I'm too busy to eat
    every up and down mood
    every sleepless night
    every friend, foe, frustration.

How do you become an adult
without the freedom to
find your own way?

24

The weather turns

cold and gray.
It feels a lot like me.

Mr. Crockett calls on me
more often in class,
as though he's trying to
remind me I'm a
contributing member
of society.

But what does a silly
high school English class
matter to the world?

Rejection after
   rejection after
      rejection
for my poems and short stories.
("I'm sorry,
   this is beautiful writing,
      but it's not right for us."
"You're clearly gifted,
   but this piece is too interior."
"It's good, but it left me wanting—
   perhaps a clearer resolution?")

I suspect Mother doesn't even

give me all of them,
since I never hear from
some of the magazines
I submitted to.

Did she hide
the Smith rejection, too?

Is it better to know
someone doesn't want you or
is it better to remain
ignorant?

25

Dark days climb on,
one after another.

"You have your whole life
ahead of you, Sivvy," Mother says.

Sometimes I get tired of
trying to fill the void.

Closing my eyes
doesn't make anything darker.
I guess that means
this is the darkest

it gets.

I wait for the shadows to
swallow me

    whole.

26

Mother comes in the door shrieking.
She's just checked the mail.
She bursts into the kitchen
while I sip my tea.

"Smith!" she says.

It's all she has to say.
I rip the envelope open.

Warren thuds into the room.
He's home for a visit from Exeter.
"What's all this?" he says.
"I thought someone was hurt—"

"What's all this?" Mother says.
"What's all this, Sivvy?"

She waits.

I haven't yet finished
reading the letter,
but I've read the most
important parts.

"I got in!" I say.

Mother shrieks again.
She takes my hands and
we jump up and down—truly!

Warren stares at us, mouth open.
"What's all this?" he says.

"What's all this?" I repeat, giggling,
Mother twirling me.
"What's all this, Mother?"

"Sivvy got into Smith!" Mother
shouts to the world.

Warren shakes his head.
"As if there was ever any doubt.
The brilliant Sylvia Plath?"

I wrap my brother in a hug.
Mother joins us.

No one mentions money.

27

I do the math.

Smith offered me a scholarship
that will pay for most of my tuition.
Mother will make up the rest.
I'll have to pay for my room and board,
but I'm fairly certain
I can do that with a job
scheduled around class time.

I wouldn't need to work
as many hours
if I chose Wellesley,
but Smith is my dream.
And you do
what you have to do
to pursue a dream.

"Are you certain?" Mother says
over a dinner of roast chicken
and baked potatoes.
She looks a little sad,
which makes me feel guilty
but also slightly scared.

How can I possibly move
so far away from them?

Maybe I can't.

But maybe I need to try.
So I say, "I'm certain, Mother."
She smiles at me like
she has no doubt in the world
that I can do this.

"You're going to be brilliant," she says.

We'll miss each other.
That's life for you.
But it's time for me to leave
and stand on my own.

I decline Wellesley
and send my acceptance to Smith.

No turning back now.

28

All the details for Smith
are arranged, but
excitement has quickly

turned to doubt,
as it so easily and often does.

Can I do this?
Will I be able to keep up?
Will I struggle to
keep my scholarship?
Will I hate being
so far from home?

What if…?

I won't allow myself to
consider silly what-ifs.
This will be an opportunity,
    a challenge,
something that will
energize me to
grab my future
with both hands.

The world awaits.
It doesn't ask whether
I'm ready to see it.

Ready or not—
            I will go.

29

High school prom tonight.

I go with Bob Riedeman.
We meet Perry Norton
and his date, Pat,
for dinner first.

I've known Perry
and his brother Dick
since we were kids.

Perry tries to initiate
conversation at the dance.
"You look nice, Sivvy," he says.
His eyes sweep my dress,
a pale pink thing with
a bow on the back.

My face gets uncomfortably hot.
"You do, too."

"You enjoying your night?" he says.

It's too warm in this room.

Pat and Bob talk

easily to each other,
which leaves Perry and me
to talk awkwardly.
They dance together, too,
which leaves Perry and me
to dance with each other.
All of that should be fine.

The problem is
Perry wanted to go as my date,
and that makes everything weird.

Why do love and friendship
have to be so complicated?

30

I sold a short story to *Seventeen*!

I practically shout
the news to Mr. Crockett.
"*Seventeen* is going to publish
'And Summer Will Not Come Again'!
This summer!"

He says, "I never had any doubt

you'd do it, Miss Plath.
This is only the beginning."

The universe is
shimmering down at me,
whispering,
>   *This is what*
>   *you were*
>   *born to do.*

31

I earned all A's this semester,
    first in my class,
but that pleasure is stolen
by a horrible disappointment.

I wasn't named
    "Best Girl Student"
in the 1950 yearbook.

Why does a silly yearbook award
matter so much to me?
It doesn't mean anything.

Barbara Botsford gets
the award instead.

   "Girl Most Likely to Succeed"
goes to Louise Giesey.
She also gets the
   "Most Outstanding Student"
award for seniors.

After the announcement,
I flee the auditorium and
duck into the bathroom.

The door opens before
I can lock myself into a stall.
I almost run right into Louise.

I turn and leave without
saying a word to her.

I don't want to hate her,
but they were supposed to be
     my awards.
I graduated at the top of my class!

At least I have
the kind and encouraging notes
from people in my yearbook.
I pull it out and write
my positive qualities
under my picture:

>Engaging smile
>Hard worker
>Skilled in chalk and paints
>Makes great sandwiches
>Good tennis player
>Future writer
>Smith girl

32

Today is graduation.

I can't help looking
at the seat next to Mother,
wishing Daddy could be here.
Times like these I miss him the most.
I imagine him saying,
Well done, darling girl.
He was never one for playing

with Warren and me
when we were children,
but he did enjoy our achievements.

I read my poem "Senior Song"
during the ceremony.
People clap. I feel...
   hardly anything.

I'm tired.

I can't help but think
this passage has now
shoved me into
the land of Old.
I am past my prime.
I've become timeworn.

Can a life

     end

before it's even

   begun?

I Must Go

Summer 1950

1

This summer I take a job
at Lookout Farm,
five miles from home.
I ride my bike
there and back.
For long, hot hours,
I pick vegetables and
clean them.

Ten weeks of work
that I hope will help
pay for college.
It's not great pay,
but it's something.

Mother hates that I'm
doing hard labor.
She thinks I won't last a week.

It's difficult to explain
how fulfilling it is
to work so near the earth,
to exhaust yourself with
picking and cleaning food,
to exist in a realm where
you don't have to impress anyone
with your thinking.

People out here
live without books.
They don't go to college.
They work.

I soak up the experience.

I write about it all.

2

Ilo is an Estonian refugee
who wants to be an artist.
He lives and works at Lookout Farm
because he needs the money to
move to New York City.

He's bronze and intelligent,
blond and muscular.
So what if he's
    fifteen years older
than me?
Age doesn't matter.

I listen to his accent
and try not to swoon.
I think he likes me, too.

He flirts,
talks music and books.
He loves Frank Sinatra.
He knows all the great German writers,
and we spend hours
discussing literature
and poetry.

I may be in love.

3

Ilo invites me
to his loft in the barn.

He wants to show me
one of his sketches.

I feel nervous going with him.
I think he might kiss me.
On the way up the stairs to his loft
we pass some other farmworkers,
and my cheeks start to burn.
I ache for the touch of
an experienced man,
but their looks remind me
I'm not supposed to.

Then he's between me and the door
and he kisses me.
I get flustered, panicked.
His arms feel too heavy,
his mouth too intense.
It's too much too soon,
and I push him away.

He stops.
He seems surprised.
"You don't…"
He lets the words
trail off.

I start crying.
It's horrifying!

"I'll get you some water," he says.
He doesn't apologize.
Do I want him to apologize?
No. It would add to my shame.
He'll think I'm a child,
acting like this.

He hands me a glass.
I don't know what to say.

"I'm sorry," he finally says.
And the shame scorches my cheeks.
"I thought we both wanted…"

I try to tell him I did want…
I felt the electric thrill of his mouth,
the pulse of his body,
and I wanted more.
But it scared me.
No one's ever kissed me
like they burn for me
the way I burn for them.

I felt alive.
    Awakened.
        Freed from the box
society built around me.

How can something be
      so wonderful
and
      so terrifying
at the same time?

He walks me out.
I bike home,
the air cool against
my flaming body.

4

Every magazine I read
frustrates me. They're filled with
glorifications of married life,
words that bid me to
     settle for wife,
    instead of poet.

I'm tired of the world

telling me what to do,
      who to be.

Words on a page
are my happiness.
I arrange them,
   shape them,
      let them loose
      into the world.
They are my children.
Publishing is my home.

How would a man
understand?

5

Two poems and a short story are
published in *Seventeen* this summer,
but I feel no sense of
accomplishment or celebration.
Instead, I feel only
a low fever of
uneasiness
   fear
      dissatisfaction.

It's happening again.
The crumbling.

Widening cracks
spider through
my belief in myself.

My stories and poems don't matter.
They're trite and unimaginative.
Why would anybody print them?
Who would read them?
Who would care?

I'll never publish in *The New Yorker*.
Seventeen plays at sophistication,
but it's nothing.

I
    am
        nothing.

6

Mother sets an envelope
on my desk. "This came
for you," she says.

I expect another rejection.
But it's a fan letter.

His name is Eddie Cohen.
He's from Chicago, twenty-one,
an English major.
He read my short story
    "And Summer Will Not Come Again"
in *Seventeen*
and was impressed.

"It was my sister's magazine," he writes,
as though to explain why a man
would read *Seventeen*.

He's a little patronizing.
But what do you expect from
a man who's also
an English major?

"It's much better than what
the magazine usually publishes," he writes.
"Very insightful, if you ask me."

I didn't ask him,
but what's so new about

a man offering his opinion
without being asked?

"Send me a story
if you like," he says.

Maybe he thinks
he can offer me
more feedback.

I write him back.
I say, "Send me something first."

I point out his patronization
in the next paragraph and
sign it, "Yours, Sylvia."

We'll see how he takes it.

You can tell a lot about a person
based on how they take
criticism.

7

Eddie writes back

but doesn't send me a story.
Maybe he doesn't trust
my editorial instincts.
He probably thinks
I wouldn't offer any
intelligent comments on it.
Or maybe he thinks I'll steal it.
Or maybe he doesn't have
a story and he lives vicariously
through the successful writers
who actually write instead of
merely talking about writing.

He does tell me about himself.
"I'm from affluent Chicago," he says,
which says a lot.
"I don't care much for that life now."

He's a junior at Roosevelt College.
He says it's a very
nontraditional school.

What does he know of tradition?
Men rarely know much,
since they don't have to care.
They benefit from tradition.

Tradition makes them gods.

I'm not sure I trust him.

8

I write Eddie back.
I suppose I'll trust him a little.

I tell him I'm
    tan,
  tall, and
    slender,
perhaps even beautiful,
but that leads to
my biggest trouble:

    Boys look at me and think
    no serious thought
    has ever troubled
    my little head.

Nearly all my thoughts
are serious.
        Take that, tradition.

9

Eddie and I have struck up
a letter relationship.
He's a very good letter writer.
I wonder if he's a good
story writer, too.

An image of him
unfolds over the weeks.
    Unconventional
    raised conservative Jewish
       but now calls himself
       spiritually independent
a cynical idealist.

He talks about sex
like it's natural,
an acceptable relational step
between two individuals.
He's candid about his
sexual adventures and
tries to convince me
sex outside marriage
isn't shameful.

But he's a man.

He doesn't *really* know
how much shame there is
for a woman,
how society heaps it on her
for doing the same things
a man does.

He acknowledges the
duplicity, though.
    "A woman has desires," he says.
    "And why shouldn't she?"

Where did this man come from?
How do we make more of them?

10

At the end of the summer,
Ilo and I say goodbye
and promise to keep in touch.

I survived my time
at Lookout Farm,
despite what Mother thought.

I feel drowned in satisfaction.

I'm stronger than Mother thinks.
And maybe that means
I'm stronger than I think, too.

11

I send Eddie some poems:
   "Bitter Strawberries,"
   "Evolution," and
   "Kitchen Interlude."
He sends me some bits of
his short stories and essays.

I can learn from him, I think.
Maybe he can
learn from me, too.

I hope he never stops writing.
I make sure I tell him so.
"So long as our relationship
remains on paper," I write,
"I think it might go on forever."

I don't want to meet him.
    Ever.
It's much easier to be candid

with a person when
you've never met them.

Things end
when people get
too close.

12

Eddie's letters distract me
from the fast-approaching
move to Northampton.
I'm not ready.

But I don't want to admit that to anyone.
For so long I've craved the freedom
I'll have at Smith—
    to leave our cramped house,
    to exist away from Mother's watchful eye,
    to live my own life apart from her.
But at the same time,
I will have to start over,
find my place and make my name,
   again, on my own.

Sometimes growing up
feels a little terrifying.

13

Resolutions:
1. I will not overcommit myself
   to any organization or club.

2. I will be educated to be educated,
   not to find a husband.

3. I will not conform.

4. I will remain myself.

5. I will cultivate time alone—
   for writing,
   for thinking,
   for simply being.

6. I will hone my talents
   and pursue my desires.

14

One day left,
and I sway.
I want to stay.
I want to go.
I don't know what I want.

Our town suffocates me.
I was made for more
than its smallness.
I desire more than
an unimaginative,
provincial life.

Northampton scares me,
with all its unknowns,
    its assured loneliness,
        its invitation to start anew
and shine on my own.
What if I don't shine?
I must still go.
I must.

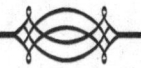

This Darkness, My Ocean

First Year at Smith, 1950–1951

1

Smith's Haven House is
   homey,
   lovely,
   small but bright.
My room's on the third floor.

I rearrange things a little.
I pull my desk in front of the window
for a better view and more light.
Both will help whether studying
or writing poetry.

I splurge on some curtains
and a wine-colored bedspread.
Now it feels like a haven
to inspire greatness.

And it's all mine.

2

Forty-eight young women
live in Haven House.
I meet several of them
in the hallways during
move-in.
Excitement thrills through me.

But there are so many girls.
And after greeting and smiling
and small-talking I feel
depleted and cranky.
So I shut my door.
Block out the world.
Lie on my bed and
listen to the clock

      tick tock tick tock

in a rhythm that calms me.

I hope the girls
forgive me
for my solitude.

3

I rally for more introductions
in the afternoon and
our cider party in
the house president's room
this evening.

Pat and Louise,
both fellow Crocketteers,
find me at the cider party.
We talk about Wellesley and
our summers and our hopes
for Smith. I've found
a little piece of home, maybe.

I didn't realize the longing
to return to the familiar
would find me so soon.

As I walk back to my room,
surrounded by new and old friends,
six hundred voices shouting and laughing,
immersing me in life,
I still can't help but feel utterly

        alone.

4

French literature
European history
Botany
English with author Mary Ellen Chase
Basic design
Physical education

My classes stimulate
and challenge me.
I spend my days studying
and reading in the library,
the kind of place where
hours slide away
peacefully and quietly.

We're required to attend chapel.
It's a lovely ritual, but
I don't believe in all that.

Today some girls
join me in my room.
We dance the Charleston together
and laugh and sing.
It's a grand time.

One girl, Ann, stays
after everyone else.
She's nearly as tall as me
and has pretty blue eyes and
short brown hair.
We spend hours talking about
God and religion
and what we believe.

I think I've found
a true friend.

5

Of all the humiliating things
a young woman must be
subjected to in her life,
this must certainly be
one of the worst.

I'm still shaking.

Apparently the girls
who come to Smith College
are required to have
a physical exam.

We had to strip naked
while nurses
took pictures of us.

Why does a school need
naked pictures of the
young women who attend?
What will they be used for?
Will they take outgoing pictures
and line them up next to
these first-week ones,
to make sure we're as
perfectly intact as
the day we came in?
If we sully ourselves,
will they revoke our diplomas?
If they find imperfections,
    blemishes,
        moles from the devil,
will they burn us
at the stake?

My attendant finds me
five foot nine inches,
one hundred thirty-seven pounds.

"Posture's decent," she says.

Another nurse says, "You tilt forward
when you stand.
Like you're about to topple over."

Which is it?

I tell myself my posture
represents me—
    ever ready for the next step forward—
and is not a prophecy of
what's to come.

I must have passed inspection,
because they let me stay.

6

These girls and
their frivolous concerns—
I want to fit in,
but I'm interested
in much more than
    dates, dates, dates.
What a hollow life!

Smith College is not

my finishing school.
My education means more.

Why pay to go to college
if you don't intend to learn
and broaden your mind and
push the boundaries of
conformity and
pursue greatness?

What will they do with
their brains when
they leave Smith?
Plan meals,
   look after children,
      keep house?

I intend to continue growing
and expanding mine.
Most of all,
I intend to use it.

7

The messages I pick up
at Smith are confusing.

My professors say
I have exceptional talent.
They encourage me to study
and develop those talents.

But most of the girls snub me.
They brand me snobbish.

What do I care?

But I find I do—
and that's the irony of it all.

How do you fight conformity
when you care so much
what people think?

8

Today I meet Enid,
a lovely girl from New York
who's published some drawings and
poems in *Seventeen*.
She's like me,
with serious ambitions
to draw and write and

be a working woman.
She scorns the hollow life, too.

We're so much alike
we can't help but be friends.

9

The days move
   up
      down
   up
      down
   up
      down

Up: Ann gets me a date
with an Amherst senior,
      Bill Gallup.
Tall, handsome,
familiar even though
we've never met.

Down: Books pile up on my desk,
work piles up in my brain,
my classes demand too much.
I might fail history

because of the reading list—
    how ironic!
We're only writing critical pieces
in English, and where does
creativity fit into that?

My teachers are exceptional,
but their expectations weigh on me.
I don't want to let them down.

No sleep,
    constantly overwhelmed,
        relentless worry about grades.
I have so much to lose!

I'm mentally and
physically exhausted.

And so I go
    up
        down
    up
        down
but mostly

        down down down

How long until
I hit bottom?

10

"You should go to bed
earlier," Mother writes.
"Sleep during your free moments.
Stop writing home with
your valuable minutes."

She's probably right.

I make a new plan:
Go to bed by ten fifteen,
don't get up before seven.

Turn chaos into order.
Maybe that's the secret to
balance.

I write out my schedule,
display it on my desk,
tell myself as soon as
I build good study habits
and better sleep routines

I'll have room to
   breathe.

11

Perhaps I could have
room to breathe...
if I could actually breathe!

I should have known
my first cold of the semester
would hit me when I'm down.
Now I've missed several classes.
I lie in bed and
worry I'll never catch up.

Bill visits me while I'm bedridden.
We've been on several dates,
but my feelings for him have cooled,
and the whole thing feels like torture.
He's so sweet and attentive,
and I'm heartless.
I don't even have the courage
to tell him I'm no longer interested.

Ann comes to see

how Bill's visit went, and
I burst into tears.

How pathetic men can make us.

Ann boils a pot of hot tea
and stays with me
until I fall asleep.

I don't call Mother.
Or crawl home.
I take a step in the direction of
learning to be
master of myself.

Isn't that what it means
to be grown up?

12

(I'm not grown up.)

Voices haunt my mind.
You'll fail at this.
   You'll go back home a disaster.
     Everyone will know
what a fraud you are.

I wander in and out of the library.
The sun hides.
Everything is gray.

(I'm not grown up.)

You'll never be a writer.
   You're nobody.
      You don't deserve
your big dreams.

I crack my books,
but no studying happens.
It's all a useless waste of time.

(I'm not grown up.)

You'll never find an intelligent man to love you.
   Everyone thinks you're strange because you study
   so hard.
      Have you seen the way
they look at you?

Time passes,

    drip drip drip

leaving me behind.

There's not time enough left
to chase my dreams.
The clock

    tick tick ticks

and I have nothing
to show for it.

Pathetic,
  flabby,
    ugly,
faceless,
  mad

    lost lost lost

13

The darkness
  of the ocean
swallows me whole.

I don't tell Mother.
I pretend all is well,
hide my depths,

fill my letters with
sunny words and hopeful lies.

    I tell myself
it's more practice
for writing fiction.

    I tell myself
she couldn't fix anything anyway—
        I've left home,
    I've grown up,
I must find my own way.

    I tell myself
this is only temporary,
but what do I know?

14

What's so wrong about
spending a weekend studying?
The girls look at me like
I'm a strange creature.

"Don't you want
to date?" Jane says.

Yes, but I also want more.
A life of my own.

"Don't you want to find
a good-looking boy
you can marry?"

Only if he believes
I'm more than a body,
I'm a brain, too.

"Don't you want to go to
the Amherst fraternity party
at Alpha Delta this weekend?"

I'm sick of these
foolish Greek names.

But I go.
You play the game
to ease the pressure.

15

The weather cools.
The sun feels like magic medicine,

lifting my spirits.
I bathe in it,
bike for hours across hills,
play tennis.
My anxious thoughts quiet.

At least until
my first English paper
returns to me with a
    B minus
marked in red.

    B minus!

If my best work
in my easiest course
is only worth a B minus,
what hope do I have
for my tough classes?

The brilliant writer
is only as good as a

    B minus.

How tragic.

16

I'm eighteen and truly an adult now.

The girls and I celebrate
my birthday at Joe's with pizza.
I try to be happy,
try to rally my excitement
to celebrate another year,
a year that launches me
fully into adulthood,
but more shadows move in
every year that passes.
     One year older,
   one year closer to death.

It's a macabre way of
looking at birthdays,
but however you slice it
time slips away.
There's so much to do!
How does a person
do it all before
it's over?

The girls don't notice
my melancholy.

I suppose I've become
an expert at playacting.
Or perhaps you grow
more invisible the longer
you're alive.

Mrs. Shakespeare,
our house mother,
meets us for a small after-party.
She asks about
my dating life,
not my educational one.

"You canceled a date so you
could study?" she says, incredulous.

I shrug.

"Sylvia." She presses a hand
over her heart.
"You shouldn't let studying
erase your social life," she says.

I socialize with the girls—
isn't that enough?

17

Miss Mensel calls me
to her office today.
She works with all
the scholarship students.

She tells me
my scholarship benefactress
is none other than the famous
Olive Higgins Prouty,
author of *Stella Dallas*.
It was a hugely successful novel
that became a film nominated
for two Academy Awards!

How amazing is that!
   My benefactress!
      A famous author!

Did she see something
special in me?
Did she recognize
a gift as impressive as hers?
Did she believe
her investment in me
would one day pay off?

It's both exciting and
terrifying to think so.

Miss Mensel doesn't seem
to notice my exhilaration.
"Sylvia," she says.
"What are you doing
with your weekends?"

"Studying," I say.
It's both true and
what I'm supposed to do.
I can't lose my scholarship
because of failing grades.
And now that I know
Mrs. Prouty is my benefactress,
I won't let her regret
her generosity.

"You shouldn't risk going stale
to spend your weekends
studying," Miss Mensel says.

What exactly does she mean?
These women talk in circles.

I know what she means:
Graduating summa cum laude

is not worth my becoming
an old maid.

If only I could agree.

18

I succumbed to
the little niggling voice
of guilt and went
on a ridiculous church date
with a lackluster boy.

When I return,
most of the girls are studying,
and I feel absolutely slothful.

You just can't win.

It's strange to consider
there are so many girls here
who are more intelligent than I am.
I don't like being mediocre.
The thought brings me
physical pain.

So I drive myself
    hard,

>   harder,
>   hardest,
> to prove that I belong here.

I deserve this.

I am enough.

19

"Ode to a Bitten Plum"
prints in this month's *Seventeen*.

Eddie, who still writes me,
has something to say about it.
Of course.

"It's overdone," he says.
"Too wordy."

Who cares what he thinks?
Where is *he* publishing?
He's just another man
offering his opinion.
The world is full of those.

Besides, it's hard to separate
his criticism from his jilted feelings.
He regularly declares his love for me,
and I regularly ignore his declarations.
We haven't even met!

He wants to meet.
He suggests it every letter.
I think it would ruin our friendship,
make it harder for me to open up to him.
He's the only person who
knows my honest thoughts!
I won't sacrifice that for some
misguided notion of love.

Men are so troublesome sometimes.

20

The published poem
restores my confidence
in English class.
No longer do I hesitate
answering questions.
I craft my essays and poetry
without agonizing over them.

I've stopped second-guessing
whether I have something
worthwhile to contribute.

I will
   speak and
      be heard.

21

Ann and I understand each other.
We want the same things—
     a career first,
   and a home, too,
if such a thing is possible.
We open our hearts to each other
and speak frankly about
anything and everything.

I don't have many friends
who see behind my mask,
but I let Ann in.
   Every dream,
     every secret,
   every fear,
every hope.

We'll take on the world
      together.

22

Ann sets me up with
Guy Wilbor, a freshman at Amherst.
He's from Chicago.
Tall, handsome, gentlemanly.
He wants to take me to
the Amherst dance.
We eat dinner first.

We talk about writing.

"My English professor
lets us write about
our personal experiences," he says.
"Creative pieces."

"What's that like?" I say.

"Interesting," he says.
"We have some interesting
experiences." He chuckles to himself.

"I want to be a fiction writer," I say.
"A poet, too."

"Oh yeah?"

I don't mention
I've been published
in *Seventeen*.

He changes the subject to
the stock market.
I ask him all about it.
He looks surprised by my interest.
I don't know whether to
laugh or feel offended.
I want to say, *You don't think
a woman can be interested
in the stock market?
Or understand the way it works?*
But I don't want to ruin
the evening.

We run into lots of
my old Wellesley friends
at the Amherst dance.

Now no one can say

all I do is
stay home and study!

23

It's peculiar,
the image you take with you
of your home when you leave it.
I don't remember home being
    this small
    this dingy
    this old.
But when I return for
Thanksgiving break,
I feel surprised by its
cramped rooms and
peeling wallpaper and
worn furniture.
How do you forget?

Mother cleaned out my room,
and now I feel like a tree
without ground to root myself in.

I spend some time with Warren
and his Exeter roommate, Clement Moore,
whose mother is Sarah-Elizabeth Rodger Moore.

A novelist! I won't get to
meet her over the holiday,
but we talk about her.

It's good to be home.

    Even so
I feel colorless and numb.
A Wellesley party and
the drive back to Smith
with some old friends
can't lift my mood.

I fear what may be coming.

24

I return to campus too soon,
before classes begin.
The days stretch out,

    endless,

no routine to them whatsoever,
and I spin in their vacancy,
end over end.

The rain pounds the windows,
   the ceiling,
      the whole earth.
It mirrors how I feel
inside.

I must get back to routine,
stop thinking so much
about myself.

I leave my room and
join a girl in the living space.
Something about the presence of
another human being
lifts my spirits.
But not completely.

My thoughts spiral.
The voice inside shouts,
   No past,
     no future,
   no present.
You may as well dispose of yourself.

But I know this darkness
   my ocean

always passes.
So I wait.

25

Exams are looming.

All I do is
    study study study.

I feel like my eyes
are about to fall out.
I read history for ten hours.
I write words I don't remember.
I examine numbers
that make no sense.

Who can bear the pace?
Who can stand the pressure?

Is this the price of greatness?

I'm burning out,
    turning to ashes.
Mother can toss them
into the sea and maybe

I'll live on like
the Little Mermaid.

26

Nothing is working out
like I expected it to.
I suppose the real problem
with caring about grades
is that when you don't
earn the marks you place
such high value on,
it devastates you.
    Splits you apart.
  Unravels you.

That's how I feel
after this first term.

Botany: A
History: A-
French: A-
English: B
Art: B-

I can't believe
I earned the worst grades
in my two best subjects.

Did I fool myself into thinking
I was a talented author and
a proficient artist?
What ridiculous, childish dreams
I had!

I suppose the real problem
with caring about grades
is they tell the truth.

27

I try to distract myself
from despondency with the
Haven House dance.
Ann doesn't have a date,
and neither do I.
We plan to ask
some Amherst boys.

I haven't been sleeping
as well as I should—
not just because of the
disappointing term grades
but also because most Saturdays
my friends and I stay out until

two-thirty or so.
I tell myself I'm young,
   I can handle it,
      it's what the young are
supposed to do,
but I feel the darkness
creeping closer again,
an ocean nipping at my toes.

My period is gone,
three months now.

It's probably stress
   lack of sleep
      worry.
I have to get things
under control.

I won't let
    the dark waters
take me under.

28

Ann tells me
she's been thinking about
suicide.

I'm shocked
by her confession.
She's depressed, and
I didn't even see it.
She's collected razor blades
and sleeping pills.

I don't know what to do.
She confided in me,
   trusted me,
     promised me
she wouldn't do it...
but do I need to write to her parents
and tell them they should
bring her home to rest?

Should I trust her promise?
Would I trust mine?

29

I check on Ann every day.
I tell her, "Get some rest.
Vacation is coming up soon.
It'll make you feel better.
One day at a time."
That's how I've learned

to keep my head above
my ocean's waves.

I make sure she throws away
her pills and razor blades.

I don't know what else I can do.

30

I had an awful date
with a World War II veteran.
I must remember
not to show such interest—
but is my interest what
gave him the wrong idea?
I simply asked him about
his experience in the war—
    did he kill anyone,
      what was it like?

Was that when he
thought I was flirting,
asking for something
I wasn't asking for?

Or was it when I said,
"What kinds of things
bother you? Hurt you?
Make you feel angry?"
I only wanted to
understand him better.

Was I too attentive?
   Too curious?
      Too forthcoming?

What made him mistake
    my kindness
  for an invitation?

He pinned me to the ground
on our walk back to campus.
I shoved him off.
We made quite a scene,
but I'm glad I kept my head.
I distracted him with more talk,
and before he knew it,
we'd arrived at Haven House.

I had a strange urge to
apologize to him.
But for what?

For not letting him do
what he so clearly wanted to do?

I know I shouldn't have agreed
to go on a night walk alone
with a man I didn't know.
But it's not my fault he overstepped.

I feel
    sick,
  small,
    confused,
ashamed.

Welcome to life as a
        woman.

31

I wasn't sure
I'd feel comfortable
with a young man
after the last disastrous date,
but Guy is different.
He asks me out again,
and I accept.

He takes me to dinner
and we ride on a sleigh,
then dance the night away.

Time off from the
pressure of school
is just what I need.

Next: Christmas vacation
and home!

32

The holiday vacation is not
the respite I envisioned.
I feel close to breaking,
mostly because of one
seemingly small realization:

> I can no longer
> lean on Mother as my
> shelter and protection.

I'm growing up.
I must handle my black moods

on my own.
She can't fix them.
It's not her responsibility.

Mother wants nothing more than
to see Warren and me happy
and fulfilled. So I'll show her
            Happy and Fulfilled Sylvia,
even if that means
    pretending that I'm perfectly all right,
        pretending there is
    no dark ocean chasing me,
pretending I'm right
where I want to be.

That all her sacrifices
have been worthwhile.

This is a daughter's gift
to her mother.

33

Months ago I wrote
a thank-you letter
to my benefactress, Mrs. Prouty.

Today I get an invitation to tea!
I don't even know what to wear!

I do know I need to
read all her novels—
immediately!

34

I keep smoothing my skirt,
making sure I have
no unsightly tears in my stockings.
Mrs. Prouty could be
the kind of person who
cares about such things.
I don't know why I'm so anxious
about this meeting, but—

What if she sees me and thinks,
    What have I done?
    Why did I choose her?
  What if she's disappointed
   in me?

What if she takes away
my scholarship and

gives it to a student who's
already well into writing
a bestselling novel?

She lives in a mansion.
I don't belong in a mansion.

But I walk up that winding driveway
and ring the doorbell. A maid—
    a real maid!—
takes me to the living room
so I can wait by the fire.
The room is painted a pretty blue,
and the windows are large enough
to let in a bright gush of sunlight
even through gold curtains.
It's the kind of room
I could imagine writing in.

Mrs. Prouty says, "Why,
you must be Sylvia!"

She sounds so excited and pleased
that I finally relax.

35

Mrs. Prouty has tea and
cucumber sandwiches
that seem just right
for the occasion.
I feel like I can be myself
in her presence.

"Have you ever written anything
about your family?" she says.

"They're just
ordinary people," I say.

"For you, perhaps.
Not for other people.
Think of the material you have there!"

I've never considered it.
I suppose I've only ever wanted
to write something important,
     something grand,
   something that shakes lives
and changes minds.

How do you do that
writing about your family?

"Writers often write stories
about the things they've
experienced," Mrs. Prouty says.
"You don't have to make everything up.
You can embellish what you already know."

I feel like she's telling me
great secrets of the
literary world.

Ideas bloom.

36

What do you think
when you read a fantastic writer,
the kind of writer who makes you
sit up and pay attention,
the kind of writer whose
turns of phrase take on
a brilliant shine?

It's probably not
what I think.

I don't think,
   This is so well done,
     what a brilliant writer,
  where can I get my hands
on their other work?

Well, I do.

But I also think,
  I will never be this great.
    I will never write so magnificently.
  I will never say something
so important so elegantly.

I want to learn from
brilliant writers,
but I doubt I can.
I want to be them,
but I'm only an imposter.
I want to try,
but I want to give up.

Why do I always feel

    less

when someone else is

    more?

37

Christmas passes in a blur,
   a few gifts,
      some money,
nothing all that special,
or maybe I'm coming down with
one of my moods again.

I go through the motions
and try to be myself.

Sometimes yourself is
the hardest person to be.

38

It's a new year.
What will this one hold?

I return to Smith
with a sinus infection,
which doesn't help things at all—
least of all my mood.

I try not to let it
set the tone for
the whole of 1951.
There has to be more than
   sickness and
   disappointment and
   loneliness
ahead. If not,
I simply don't know if
I can bear it.

I find out Ann's
not coming back.

She was my one *real* friend here,
the only one who understood me.
We were supposed to room together.
We were supposed to spend
long hours talking and
reading and writing.
Who will save me from
the winds of gossip now?

How can I be me
without Ann here?

I'm a shell of myself.
I hope she's more than a shell.
I hope she gets
what she needs at home.

39

I'm despondent.
I open my journal
and try to write,
close it again,
    empty like me.
Not a coherent thought
to share.

I know I'm lucky to be here.
I know a million girls would
trade places with me.
I'm a student at one of the
best colleges in the country.

What do I have to complain about?

Still I fall and fall and fall.

40

Small things keep me
afloat.

An A minus on my English assignment.
"Den of Lions" wins third prize
in *Seventeen*'s fiction contest.
The magazine will publish it
this summer.
I'll get one hundred dollars.

Little by little,
I'm pulled back up.

41

Maybe Ann's absence
is for the best. I might never have
ventured out in search of distractions
if we'd holed up in our room,
reading and writing all the time.
Think of the experiences
I might have missed!

I might not have met Marcia.

She's completely alive.
She shares my opinions about life.
We talk them over
on long walks in the biting cold.
We have philosophical conversations
about who we want to be and
what society wants from us and
how we'll defy traditional expectations.

She's another person
who understands me.

Is there anything better
in all the world than to
simply be understood?

42

Marcia and I skip the winter carnival.
Her roommate is away,
so I stay with her.
We hike through nature
and share meals.

Who needs boys
when you have a friend?

43

Dick Norton writes me a letter.
Three whole pages.
He'll graduate from Yale this year
and plans to head to
Harvard Medical School.

I've known Dick since we were kids,
but he's never shown much interest in me.
His brother Perry was a good friend.
Perry even writes me sometimes.
This is the first letter from Dick.

"I wondered if you'd be interested
in coming to Yale for a weekend
in February," he writes.
"We could tour the campus
or walk into town."

It doesn't matter what we do;
I'm thrilled by the invitation.
Dick is just the sort of boy
I'd like to get to know better:
    medical student
    handsome

intelligent
ambitious.

I write back an enthusiastic

      yes!

44

My period comes back,
after five months missing.
I wonder if it means
the stresses of my first year
are starting to stabilize.

But I find out Mother has an ulcer.

She worries too much.
About me,
   Warren,
     the future,
  money.

I write her a letter
and tell her,
  "Your Sivvy is doing swell!"

My letters will be a story I tell
to keep her healthy.

45

I spend the weekend with Dick.
It pours on Saturday,
so we stay in his room
most of the day.
He's living with a
Yugoslavian refugee who was
once in the Hitler Youth
but now disavows it.

I'm so nervous
I feel like I need
some cocktails
to give me courage,
but of course Dick
doesn't like girls who drink.
So I don't ask.

Dick shows me some of
his old sociology papers—
he visited a mental institution once!

I read some of his poetry.

I want something more to happen,
but he doesn't even try to kiss me.
I'm sure Dick likes his girls
chaste and passionless.

I try not to feel stupid
and dim around him.
He's studying to be a doctor,
and I'm, what?
 A poet?
He's mastered math and science
and I have only a slight skill—
in liberal arts.

I start to say something
and swallow it.
I question everything.
I don't think a single thought
in my head
is worth saying out loud.

How could I date someone
who makes me feel so foolish?

46

Dick invites me to
the Yale prom,
and I decide to give him
another chance.

Maybe I can dazzle his friends
and that will make me
feel better about myself.

47

I look like Cinderella.
My white gown
hangs off one shoulder
and clings to my figure.
It makes my brown eyes
stand out.
I borrow some things
from the girls:
    an old fur coat,
        a crinoline,
               silver sandals.

I feel a bit pieced together,

but Dick doesn't seem to notice.
He dances like a dream.

After the dance he walks me
up the hill toward the house
where I'm staying, and
we stop and listen to the wind.

I swear something changes,
unfolds between us.

Am I
falling in love?

48

The day after the dance
Dick and I go for a bike ride.

It's long and cold and exhausting
but exhilarating.

We write a letter to Mother together.
He flatters me. "Sylvia was
the prettiest girl in the room," he writes.
"She easily outshone the others."

"I'm going to take her to a play," he writes.
"I hope it's not too much
for a young lady after
two full days already."

Patronizing words,
but I dismiss them.
Maybe he doesn't have
the grasp of language I do.
He probably doesn't intend it
to sound so...insulting.

I almost say, *Women aren't
as weak as you think.*
But I stay quiet.

49

It's technically spring break,
but I won't have a ride home
until Mother comes tomorrow.

I walk into the living room
at Haven House and see

a dark-haired boy with
a pipe stuck between his teeth.

He says, "This is the third dimension."
Like we're in a play.
Or this is a joke.

It's Eddie.

How many times
have I told him
we cannot meet in person?
How many times
have I said
it would ruin everything?

Eddie has ruined

        everything.

50

"I've come to drive you
home for break," Eddie says.

I'm a fool.
"Okay," I say.
I toss my suitcases into his Nash,
which he borrowed from his father.

"I thought it would give us
some time to talk
in person," Eddie says.
I don't even look at him.

We barely speak on the way home.
It's too awkward, being with this boy
who knows all my secrets.
He's a stranger, but he's not.
I try to imagine he's just
some taxi driver off the street.
I try to imagine he doesn't
know more about me than
most of my girlfriends do.

The drive feels like endless agony.
I can hardly keep still,
I'm so nervous.

I peek at Eddie from
the corners of my eyes.

He keeps his fixed on the road.
I wonder if he feels as
uncomfortable as I do.

I told him we should never meet.
I warned him this would happen.
Men are so stupid!

51

We make it home.
I don't invite Eddie inside.
I don't want to explain
everything to Mother.

I should have invited him in.
Mother's cross—
but she's not cross
that Eddie showed up.
She's cross at me and
my inhospitality.

"How could you send him away
without inviting him in?" she says.

I regret not offering him
a cup of coffee before
he drove all the way back
to Chicago.

But what would we have
talked about, face-to-face?
The hours of silence in the car
answered that question.
We've given away too much
of ourselves on the page.
There's nothing left
outside of our letters.

52

Dick shows the
May edition of *Seventeen*
to all his Yale friends.
"Den of Lions" is in it.
He passes along their compliments,
which puff me up.

"I'm so proud of my girl," Dick writes.

Other friends send
congratulations, too.

Eddie's note is annoying, though.
"It feels like it's trying too hard," he writes.
As if he's ever had anything
published in *Seventeen*.
As if he's an expert
or something.

I reread the story.
It makes me sick.
I think Eddie's right.
It's maddening how
insightful he can be.
When I wrote the story months ago,
I thought it was the greatest thing
I'd ever done. Now
it's bleeding sentimentality.
How does one ever
publish anything?

53

I visit Dick at Yale
most weekends.

We browse bookstores and
ride bikes and
read Hemingway out loud.

He sends letters between our visits.
He wants me to teach him
how to write poetry.
He thinks we could be
a creative team.

I won't say I'm in love.

But I am rather close.

54

Betty is already engaged.
She'll marry in June.
She's my age!
I can't imagine it!
There's so much more
life to live before marriage.

The pressure to marry
will increase in the coming years.
I know that.
Every young woman knows it.
We're in our prime.

And our prime
doesn't last long.

55

Dick writes to Mother often.
He calls her Aunt.

Is that strange?

It feels like pressure.
I can't be honest with Mother
about Dick now.

Why is love so complicated?

56

Final exams are done!
Now I have three months
of freedom in front of me.

Perry and Dick drive me
back to Wellesley.
The whole trip, Dick explains

carboxyl and hydroxyl groups.
I try to pay attention.

Is this what we'll talk about
in the future?
I'm not sure I'll manage
to stay awake!

Impossible to Be a Woman

Summer 1951

1

Summertime is
    Faulkner,
Woolf,
    Steinbeck,
Auden,
    Pearl Buck.

Summertime is
  soaking up sun,
    writing Marcia,
  penning silly poems.

Summertime is
  lazy days,
  dreaming,
    recuperation.

2

Dick calls.
"Some friends and I are
going on some trips together," he says.
"So I won't be home
for a few weeks."

"Oh." I try not to let
    my disappointment
bleed into the words.

I thought attending
his commencement would
seal our relationship.
He seems to be pulling away.

Glimpses are all I get.

At the same time,
I'm tired of trying to
read into his words and
figure out his moods.
Maybe some distance
will be good for us.
I'll try not to care
what he's doing.

I'll have a grand summer
by the sea.

My happiness
does not depend on
a stupid boy.

3

While Dick is gone to Maine,
I visit the town tennis courts.
I run into Phil McCurdy.
He's a senior at Bradford Senior High
and plays tennis for the school.
I've known him for four years,
but, boy, has he changed!

He lives three blocks away.
We used to sneak out together
to look at the stars.

I'm not sure what to think
about my attraction—
he's a younger man.
And there's Dick.
But Dick doesn't own me.

After our friendly games,
I pat him on the shoulder
and say, "You should
come see me sometime."

The next move is up to him.

4

This summer, instead of
working at Lookout Farm,
I'll babysit the Mayo children—
    two-year-old Joanne,
    four-year-old Pinny,
    and six-year-old Freddy—
until Labor Day.
The job pays well,
    twenty-five dollars a week,
and I'll also stay with them
and eat with them.
I'll have one day off
every week.

What's even better:
Marcia will be watching

the children of Mrs. Mayo's sister
just down the road.

Dick's back from his travels,
so we drive to Swampscott,
where the Mayos live,
to see where I'll spend
the rest of my summer.
The house sits on top of a hill,
so near the sea you can probably
feel its splashes from the porch.

There's a tennis court on the grounds
and a yacht out in the harbor.

What would it be like
to have such money?

I can't believe
I'll be living in this world.
I can't wait.

5

Children are hard work.

I assumed I'd have
an easy time, spend my days
walking the beach and
swimming when I wanted
and writing poems
when inspiration hit me
and occasionally tending
to the children.

I have an enormous room
that opens up to the sea,
a perfect space to write.

But I do no writing.
The children demand
every second of my time.

I help with their
baths and bedtime.
Pinny has night terrors.
Joanne wakes at five in the morning.
I don't get enough sleep.
And then the day begins.

Pinny and Freddy fight,
and while I'm calming them both down

Joanne stuffs her mouth with sand.
It's too much for one person!

As if that's not enough,
Mrs. Mayo has me
washing and folding laundry
and making beds while
trying to keep children alive,
and there is not enough of me
to go around.

    On their own,
the Mayo children are darlings.
    Together,
they're completely unmanageable.

I look forward to
hiding in the cellar,
washing the mountain of laundry
that piles up every day.
Who would have ever thought
I'd say such a thing?!

6

Well, the Mayos don't just
expect me to

watch the children
do laundry
mop the floors and
make the beds.
They also want me to prepare
all the children's meals.

I don't even know how to cook!
Mother never made me
work in the kitchen.
I scorch soup and burn bread.
I have no idea how to
chop vegetables without
cutting myself.

If Mrs. Mayo catches me
reading while the children nap
she says, "Perhaps you should
try a new recipe."

I get no breaks.
I work fourteen hours a day.

What does she do all day?

7

My expectations were
too high, I suppose.

I thought I'd be treated
as part of the family.
I didn't realize I'd be
a lowly maid or governess.

I'm in college.
I'm a Smith girl.
I thought that meant
    something.

I was wrong.

A woman's sphere has
too many limits.

8

I'm trapped in a place
I can't stand.

Dick's waiting tables
in Cape Cod, but
I can't go see him.

My face is a mess.
I haven't slept in so long
my eyes look sunken and shadowed.
I've lost my beauty.

I'm so dead at
the end of my day
      eight p.m.
that I go straight to bed.

All those plans I made
with Marcia—gone.
There's no time. No break.
No relief.

No one here to talk to.
No one here to see.
No one here to remind me
who I am and that
this won't last forever.

I'm trapped in a place
I can't stand

           with no way out.

9

Three weeks in,
I nearly quit.

But a whisper stops me.
*You'll feel trapped in
your little room in Wellesley, too.
Remember how smothering
it is to be home? What it's like
to exist without routine and purpose?
At least you have your own space here.
At least you're making money.*

I think about what Mrs. Prouty told me.
*Writers often write stories
about the things they've experienced.*
I tell myself I can survive
by writing about the Mayos.

Writing can help me survive
     anything.

10

The Mayos leave
on a weeklong cruise.

They ask me to stay and
watch the house.
Of course I say yes.

I imagine myself
the mistress of the place.
I swim,
    play the piano,
        unwind on the porch,
    bathe in the sun.
It's blissful to be
    alone and
        alive.

And then they come home,
and I am once again
crushed under the machine of
their endless expectations.

11

Marcia has a much better time
at her house than I do.
She doesn't have to cook or clean.
She invites me to parties

she has time to attend,
but I have too much work.

We spend a few days off together
    (finally!)
tanning on the beach.
I've met some local boys,
but it's not like I have time to date.

Marcia's boyfriend
    Mel Woody
is literary. I have to admit,
I'm a little jealous. He sends her
regular letters full of poetry.

What do I get from Dick?
A lengthy, boring explanation
of how the body contains
six hundred fifty muscles
that have specific functions
including blah blah blah blah blah.

12

It almost makes me sick
how much wealth there is

in the world for a select few,
while the rest of us struggle
for a living.

Eleven rooms on the Mayos' yacht!
We don't even have eleven rooms
in our house.

They have a cabin boy
who can decorate cakes.
Why do they need a cabin boy
who can decorate cakes?

What do rich people do all day?

I write at night,
my fingers blistered and cut
from the ironing and cooking I do
so they can live their life of ease.

What a world.

13

I'm not sure
I like who I am
with children.

I hear echoes of Mother
in the things I say
to the Mayo kids.
I see her face growing from mine.
It frightens me.

When you don't want to
become your mother,
who do you become?

Mother didn't teach me how to
manage simple household tasks.
She's pushed me toward relationships,
hoping I'll marry.
She tried to shelter me from unhappiness,
and that made me incapable of
dealing with unhappiness.

I think I may hate her.

What kind of daughter
hates her own mother?

14

Mel hitchhikes all the way
to Swampscott from New Jersey

so he can visit Marcia.
The three of us spend
a day at the beach.
He reads aloud from Rilke's
Sonnets to Orpheus.

His voice is rich and mesmeric.
But even that doesn't
move me like it should.

I haven't been able to write
anything of consequence lately.
It's weighing me down.
My brain feels closed to me,
poetry like an enemy.

I confess it to Mel.

"So stop writing," he says.
"Give up."

Give up writing?
Does he even know
what he asks?
    It's impossible!
   It would kill me!
I would live with no purpose!

I write because
there is a voice within me
that will not be still.

I don't say a word to him.
I walk into the sea.
I swim so far I can
barely see the shore.

Mel follows me.
"Sylvia!" he yells.
"Come back!"

I don't come back.
I keep swimming.
I swim so far my arms
feel like deadweights.
I'm not sure I'll make it back.
It doesn't matter.

"I won't swim any farther," Mel says.
"I can't. Please turn around."

I almost don't turn around.

But the sun promises something
in that moment. It says,
*This isn't how you become great.
Remember?*

So I turn around.
And save my life and Mel's,
in one thousand strokes.

15

I haven't heard from Dick.
I worry he's forgotten me.
I worry he's working with
some beautiful waitress who can
seduce him with a look.
Men are such fragile creatures.
A pretty face or form is enough
to ignite their lust.

What do I care?
Maybe I want someone else.
I'll go out on exciting dates.
Let him know he has
no power over me.

I won't do anything of the sort.
He has Mother on his side,
and I know what I must do.
I must stop flirting with the
lifeguards at beach parties.
Stay true to Dick.

A whisper slides in:
*Perhaps you don't really
love him.*

I won't let myself consider
the possibility.

16

Dick finally visits.

We bike to Marblehead.
It rains. My desire ignites
and has nowhere to go.
He leaves, with barely a peck.

What do you do with
bottled-up desire?
I need some stimulating activity.

I decide to go swimming.
The water's warm from the rain.

Mrs. Mayo says, "Why would you
swim at this hour? In this weather?"
She disapproves.

What do I care?
I have twelve days left.

I can do as I please.
   I am my own person.
      I belong to no one but myself.

17

There's no denying that
I've grown in my job with the Mayos.

I didn't know how to
cook eggs when
the summer began.
Now I can make my own
   applesauce
   date-nut bars
   lamb chops.
The children do what I say

and love me.
I think I'm rather
good at this after all.

But something needles at me.
Mrs. Mayo serves Mr. Mayo—
even women with money can't escape
conventional expectations.
It's a man's world.

What a tragedy,
being born a woman.

I want to do what
men are able to do—
    spend time in bars,
      sleep in fields,
   walk around at night
without feeling afraid.
I want a man's world.

Dick will never accept
that part of me. He'll never
be content with a woman
who has no desire to cook for him
or fold up her mind in disuse

or hear about life secondhand
instead of experiencing it herself.

Dick expects
a Mrs. Mayo.

18

I write to Eddie about my fears,
like I always do.
He's the kind of friend
who can make me feel better,
    less out of my mind,
  more centered.

"A woman in our society
has a very clear social role," he says.
"Home, kids, dinner every night.
For most of the men you know,
that's their expectation."

"Conventional morality," he calls it.
What an ugly term.
And yet he's not wrong.
How I wish he was.

Maybe it's impossible
to have a family *and* a career.
And if that's true...

Maybe I need to let Dick go.

19

Dick invites me to spend
a long weekend on the Cape.

I don't want to,
for lots of reasons—
    doubts included.
But especially because Mother's going,
and so are Dick's parents.
Not exactly scintillating company.

I accept the invitation anyway.

Mr. Norton pontificates about
Pilgrim history on the drive
and even stops off at Plymouth Rock.
"Bow your head at the shrine," he says.

I do what he says.
Don't ask me why.

I feel like I'm bowing to
commercialized patriotism.
It takes every ounce
of my restraint to
stop myself from
bursting into laughter.

American mythmaking
is alive and well,
in case anyone forgot.

20

Perry comes along to the Cape,
since his parents
rented the cottage.

I'm so glad to see him.
Dick obviously is not.

I find myself gravitating
more toward Perry instead of Dick.

I tell myself it's because
Dick has been aloof lately.

I run off to the beach with Perry.
When we're alone,
he touches my face,
    my back,
  my hands.

"You're beautiful," he says.
"And brilliant. You know that, Sivvy?"

"I could use a reminder," I say.

He sits up. "The world is
brighter with you in it."

"Is it?"

"How could you ever doubt it?"
He looks at me so deeply
I feel like I'm stripped bare.
Like a starved little girl,
begging for scraps.
I want to hear him say it all again,
but I don't ask.

"My world is brighter
with you in it," Perry says.
He leans his head on mine.
I want to kiss him, but
he jumps to his feet and
holds out his hand.
"Care for a swim?"

Have I chosen the wrong brother?
Maybe it's not too late
to fall in love with
Perry.

21

Perry and I take long evening
walks together during the vacation
while Dick is... I don't know where.
We kiss a few times,
but I think we're both feeling
doubtful that this will go anywhere.
Perry has a girlfriend.
And I have Dick.

"Let's be lifelong comrades
and confidantes," Perry says.

I agree.

It's a strange relationship, I know.
But I won't feel guilty about it.
I feel closer to Perry than to Dick.

What's so wrong with that?

22

Dick remains distant
during our long weekend.

Maybe he suspects
something is happening
between Perry and me.

For three days we barely
look at each other.

Finally, I can't bear
the silence anymore.
I catch him alone on the beach.

"Weather's nice today," he says.

"It's a little hotter than I'd like," I say.
And then I'm furious with

myself and him,
for making small talk.

The anger consumes my next words.
"I didn't come here to
talk about the weather."

Dick looks up.
I can see the confusion
on his face, probably
put there by my fiery tone.

"You haven't talked to me
in three days!" I say.

Dick traces something in the sand,
but I can't read it. He says,
"I'm sorry, Sivvy. We'll talk tonight.
After dinner."

I'm not sure my nerves
can handle the wait.

23

After dinner Dick and I
head toward the fields.

We lie down under
a diamond sky.

He misunderstood my last few letters.
"I thought you weren't interested
in me any longer," he says.

"What gave you that idea?" I say.

He shrugs. "The tone?"
He sounds uncertain.

"You know I'm not overly sentimental."

"You can be."

Does that mean I must be, for him?

"I'm sorry," he says. "All this time."

We make up for the loss of
minutes and hours and days and weeks.
A whole month of misinterpretation.
He calls me darling as he kisses me.
He says he loves me as he touches me.
He whispers he wants to marry me
as he lowers me back onto the sand.

I'm not sure if my happiness
is real or manufactured.

I should probably know
a thing like that,
   shouldn't I?

24

Dick said the M word.

Most girls would be thrilled.
  Am I?

Hell no.

I spend the next day wondering.
Do I love him?
I don't know.
Do I want to marry him?
I don't know that, either.
I'd be a doctor's wife.
That seems like a cage of its own.

I just don't want
 a home and a husband and children
more than I want anything else.

More than I want
    a life and a career and writing.

I don't want to be less.
I want to be more.

But will I regret it later,
if I don't marry while
I'm young and beautiful?
The option will one day go away.
And what if I change my mind?

Why is it so impossible to be
a woman?

25

On the way back to Wellesley,
Mother and Mrs. Norton
sit in the back, which leaves me
to sit beside Mr. Norton.
I wish Perry or Dick were here,
but they already drove back to school.

"You know we would love
for you to be our
daughter-in-law," Mr. Norton says.

He's saying more than he's saying.

He's saying, *Dick would
provide well for you.*
He's saying, *Dick's marrying
beneath him, but
we're okay with that.*
He's saying, *Just think of the life
you could have with
my golden boy.*

It makes me feel like crying.
   Or screaming.
      Or fleeing.

So many people
will be happy if this works out.
But what about me?

A Succession of Little Hells

Second Year at Smith, 1951–1952

1

I'm on the second floor
of Haven House this term,
and Marcia's back.
We're rooming together.

We decorate our bedroom
in dark green and white.
We have bookcases lined with books
and a Georgia O'Keeffe picture
hanging on the wall.

It looks like a home.
The kind of room where
great writing happens.

2

I'm taking five yearlong classes this term:

Introduction to Politics
Introduction to Religion
Nineteenth- and Twentieth-Century Literature
Visual Expression
Practical Writing with Evelyn Page
along with physical education—
dance one semester, sports the other.

I sign up to join the Press Board,
which will allow me to write
for different newspapers.
I want my first story to be
about the local mental hospital.

No Saturday classes,
which means I can
use that time to write and
submit to magazines.

This will be a good year.

3

Dick writes me regularly.

His letters are clearly from a
Harvard Medical School student.

He includes gruesome details
about X-rays and cadavers.
He sends anatomical drawings.
Includes lecture snippets.
I know I said I wanted to learn
more about his world,
but does he really think
this intrigues me so much
that I'll read the entire letter?

I don't. I skim.

He invites me to
a pathology lecture on
one of my precious Saturdays.

No thank you.

I decline and read instead.

4

Dick says he ignores
flirty nurses.
I didn't ask him to.

I, for one,
will take all the male attention
I can while I can.

It will help me figure out
if Dick is truly someone
I want to marry.

Maybe there's
an artist or poet out there
waiting for me.

5

Maureen Buckley's having
a debutante ball.
She's invited everyone
at Haven House.
She's also invited some smart
    (and hopefully
        devastatingly handsome)
young men from Yale, Amherst,
and Princeton.

The Buckleys are like the Kennedys—
    intelligent, rich, and good-looking.
I have a feeling I'll meet
someone remarkable
at this party.

I don't invite Dick.
It's not my party, after all.

6

The Buckley home is extravagant.
I've never seen wealth like this.

Girls in elegant gowns
cluster everywhere.
I catch Marcia's eye.
She's wearing a lovely lilac dress.
We smile at each other.

Waiters serve champagne.
We eat and dance and laugh.

Mother would be happy to see this.
Her daughter on the way up.
Her daughter looking gorgeous.

And then I see him:
   a magnificent dark-haired boy
      grinning at me from across the room.

He introduces himself:
Constantine Sidamon-Eristoff.
He's a Georgian prince!

An actual prince!

We dance for hours,
then leave the party and
walk on the lawn.
We talk and laugh and
I don't feel the least bit afraid
to show my intelligence or
share my dreams or
be who I am.

He kisses my hand.
I don't want the night to end.

But of course
every night must.

7

"Shall I take you
home?" Constantine says.

"Yes!" I try to sound calm,
but my insides are quaking.

We talk of his past on the drive.
I recite poetry.
Wind blasts through
our open windows.

"Don't suffocate
in my hair!" I say.

"A divine way
to die," he says.

When we drive up to the mansion
where I'm lodging for the night,
he says, "Stay where you are."
He gets out of the car and
crosses to my side.
He opens the door and
holds out his hand.
"Milady," he says.
I curtsy.

No good-night kiss,
but that means nothing.

He's a prince.
    A gentleman.

I have exquisite dreams
all night.

8

Dick visits five days after
the enchanting night
at the Buckleys'.

I know now that
I'm not in love with him,
but still I can't end things.
He's a safety net. Or perhaps
it's more than that.
Pressure from his family.
Pressure from my mother.
Pressure from the world.

We canoe on Paradise Pond
and lunch at the Yankee Pedlar
and end our night at Joe's
for pizza and beer.

We don't have a terrible time.

But how does anything compare
with a night with a prince?

9

School exhausts me,
less than two months in.
My classes are so much more
challenging than last year's.

I'm reading the Romantic poets
in literature, but I feel like a fool.
I can't understand a thing.

I tell myself it's
the sinus infection.
I tell myself it will get easier.
I tell myself at least I can write.

I've sent a story to *Seventeen*.
I get a fan letter from
a woman in Hong Kong
who read one of my poems.

Nothing is enough
to lift this ocean of darkness.

10

I'm almost glad to have
a sinus infection, since
it gives me a reason to
cancel a weekend with Dick.

How many excuses
will I have to fabricate
before I have the courage
to end it once and for all?

11

Constantine invited me to Princeton!

I can hardly keep from shrieking.
The girls swarm around me.

"He hasn't forgotten me!" I tell them.

Marcia squeezes me tight.
"Who could forget you, Sivvy?" she says.

The trip will be expensive.
But I must go. I must!

This could be my emancipation.
Constantine is a prospect.
He's the only boy I've met after Dick
whom I could imagine
spending my life with.

I must at least see
where it will lead.

12

Wisdom has won the day.

I cancel my trip to see Constantine.
I simply have too much work to do.
And what is more important:
    My professional future,
        or my marriage future?

I've made my choice.

13

Dick, Marcia, and I celebrate
my nineteenth birthday.

They give me books by T. S. Eliot
and e. e. cummings.
We read poetry out loud
and drink bottles of Chianti.

But darkness creeps in.

I can't stop myself
from drawing a gravestone
on a letter to Mother.
I write, "Life was a hell of
a lot of fun while
it lasted."

14

Guess what I've learned.

Holier than thou,
   mighty,
      perfect Dick
is not a virgin!

He confessed to me
over Thanksgiving break.

What hypocrisy!

So he expects to marry
a virgin wife—
      pure, unsullied—
but he has already
had his fun?

I feel sick.

He teased *me* for being
wise about sex, knowing
more than perhaps he thought
I should know.
And now this?

I know my anger is ridiculous.
I know every other boy in the world
is exactly like Dick. They live by
double standards.

I would have gladly slept with
many of the boys I dated,
if I wasn't such a coward.
Afraid of the consequences and
   the way the world looks at

women
    who follow their desires.

I won't let him
trap me into marriage.
I have a bigger future:
    continuing my education
    and writing and publishing.
He's too
    rational and scientific
for me anyway. I'm
    artistic and passionate.
It never would have worked
between us.

How will I tell him
we don't fit?

15

I'm worn out.
Life is too much.

I can't sleep.
My period plagues me.

I'm living a succession of
little hells,

day after day after
day.

16

Constantine again invites me
to visit Princeton.
It's hard not to see it as a sign.

I spend the first part of
    the holiday break
visiting Marcia's family in New Jersey,
then meet Constantine in New York.
We eat dinner at his family's apartment
on the Upper East Side.
His parents and grandmother
are there.

It's delightful.
They welcome me like
a member of their family.
I can hardly contain my glee.

After dinner,
we drink and dance
at a Russian bar.

I feel sexy and strong
and beautiful and fun.

What a difference to
my time with Dick.
No anatomy clinics.
No boring talks.

And kisses.

17

I'm back at Smith, and
Constantine goes silent.
Dick is here.
So I take him.

Maybe I won't always
feel so indecisive.
I'm just keeping
my options open.

Sometimes I wonder,
    Options for what?
        A future?
    I don't need a man to have
a future worth living.
      I might want to love a man,
        I might want a man,
    but I certainly don't need one.

Why do I prolong a relationship
I don't really want?

It's partly Mother's fault.
She loves Dick like a son.
It's difficult to leave him
when Mother is constantly
singing his praises.

And Dick loves her.
He takes her on tours of hospitals
and on medical expeditions
and writes to her
as faithfully as he writes to me.
Isn't that strange?

Perhaps he should marry
Mother instead.

18

I don't feel refreshed
after break this time around.
I only hope I can hold on
until spring vacation
without losing my mind.

Marcia's sick with a cold,
so our room is a wreck.
It's not all her fault.
I'm sinking into my ocean,
and she's too sick to pull me out.
Neither of us clean or tidy.
The room reflects our ruined selves.

I feel old and frumpy and
unattractive and wound up tight.
Smith expects too much of us.
I expect too much of myself.

Seventeen rejects a story.

I know this business
is full of rejections.
But you can know that and
still feel the slap every time

one reaches you.
You can still watch
the fragile dream shatter
like it's made of fine glass.

Will it always feel this way?

19

Eddie's a comfort
in my darkness.

I write, "I know I'm not pretty enough.
I don't have enough money.
Men don't seem to understand me.
Sometimes I hate myself."

He writes back and says
I have no good reasons
to hate myself.
"Anybody would love
to be you," he says.

"I ache for sex.
I feel dirty for it," I write.

He says my desire is normal.
I'm just living in a society
that denies it exists.

I tell him about Dick.

"Break it off," he writes.
"You deserve better."

I can't argue.
What would I do
without Eddie?

20

Today I hear an
inspiring sermon on
love and marriage.
The pastor says,
"Don't marry
until the right partner
comes along."

"Wait and work after college," he says,
"so you can enrich yourself
and figure out who you want to be."

I've never heard
a holy man say that.
I take it as permission.

So many friends are
announcing engagements.
I don't want to be one of them.

I write Mother about
what the pastor said.
I hope in my letter she hears that
I don't want to marry Dick.

21

Dick writes to say
he can't wait to spend
all our future days together
reading poems and plays.
He says he loves Faulkner,
    Chaucer,
        Hemingway,
    Emerson,
        Melville,
    Goethe.

He invites me to
literary readings.

We talk Auden on a date—
    for seven hours.
We don't even eat.

He writes me love letters.
He dances with me in
the Northampton streets
after the Smith formal.
He wants to read
Wallace Stevens together.

He's trying so hard
it makes me feel awful.

I will not give up
    my art
for a man
I do not love.

No woman should.

22

Constantine invites me
to the Princeton prom.

I have to decline.
It's too expensive,
and I have too much work.
I don't want to exhaust
myself again.
I don't want
    the riptide
that always follows.

It feels like the end of
a possibility.

23

Room and board at Smith
is going up
    one hundred fifty dollars
next year.
Another worry to add
to my list.

I'll have to spend
the summer working
  again
as a nanny or a waitress.

Money's the worst.

24

Why am I so hard on myself?

I'm nominated
for house president and the electoral board.
I'm voted the honor board secretary.
I make Alpha Phi Kappa Psi
and get elected to a committee
comprised of the best leaders
in each class.

Why do I assume
no one likes me?

People treat me like
a celebrity. I'm known
as a published writer,
a straight-A student.

I've had a few literary
accomplishments, I suppose.
But it's still not enough.

Will it ever be?

25

I write more poems than
I have in a long time.

I send some to Eddie.

He writes, "Your poems
made me gasp. I feel things,
big things." He calls me
"one of the
      great creative geniuses
of our generation."

Could he be right?

26

When I go home for spring break,
it's clear Mother and I are
growing further and further apart.

"How can you believe
there's no afterlife?" she says.

"There just isn't," I say.

"You don't go to church?"

"It's a man-made institution.
I'm an agnostic humanist."

"But you do go to a church," she insists.

"It's Unitarian," I say.
"And it's not really a church."

"What do Unitarians believe?"

"They believe that
the Bible is literature and that
Jesus was a human, not a god."

She stares at me blankly.
I think I've broken Mother.

27

I write what I consider
my greatest creative work
of the year during the break.
I take my experience by the sea
and my relationship with Dick

and turn it into a short story.
I call it: "Sunday at the Mintons'."

    Henry
is inflexible and mulish.
His sister
    Elizabeth
is erratic and impulsive.
He confines her, and she resents him.

The story is
my message to Dick.

I hide my greatest fears
in the words, and I hope
he'll be able to decode them.

It's easier than coming out
and saying:

    A future with Dick
    might choke the life
    out of me.

28

Dick joins me for
Smith's sophomore prom.

We spend nearly every
weekend together.
We keep up the farce
     (me)
and fall deeper in love
     (him).

We do everything-but.

My desire is large and desperate.
It's not about him;
it's about my body.
We can hardly tear ourselves apart.

I don't know how much longer
I'll be able to resist.
I know it will make
breaking up harder,
but why shouldn't I get
what I need while I can?

29

The semester's done.
Mother drives me back to Wellesley.

My only Bs were in art and
physical education.
At least I excelled in
the classes that mattered this year.

I feel on top of the world.

But every time
I feel on top of the world,
I wonder how much
the fall down will hurt.

Because the fall down always comes.
It's only a matter of time.
It's a shadow hanging over
everything.

I try to enjoy
each day like it's
my last.

Up, Down, Sideways

Summer 1952

1

I don't know why
I agreed to spend my
first weekend of summer break
with the Nortons.
Every hour I spend with Dick
makes it harder to leave
for good.

I'm a coward.
   Terrified of being alone.
      Terrified of not being alone.

How do you
reconcile the two?

2

Eddie comes to visit.
This time he asked.

We walk around Lake Waban.
He drives me places
in his coral convertible.
He's probably trying to impress me.
It doesn't work.

We talk about life and love.
It gives me the perfect opportunity
to say, "You know a romantic relationship
between us will never happen."

He nods. "I know."

"I value our friendship too much.
You know too much about me.
You're like…" I try to find
the right words. "A wise brother
who challenges me to be
better than I am."

"A brother," he says.
He looks disappointed.
But he had to know
this was coming.

I shrug.

"Okay," he says.
"A brother it is."

It's a great relief.

3

Today I start my job
at the Belmont.

It's a fancy resort
on West Harwich beach.
I'll live in the women's dorm
and work three two-hour shifts
every day. At night
I plan to party out on the beach.

They assign me to
the staff dining room.
I have to serve my employers,
which is not what I expected.
A little humiliating, and no tips.

I'd hoped for a glimpse
of the high life and to meet
a rich, handsome boy.
But I'm hidden away.

Maybe it's for the best.
I still haven't officially left Dick.

4

On my work break I get
a telegram from Mother.
"Sunday at the Mintons' " won
first prize in the
Mademoiselle fiction contest!
I'll get five hundred dollars!

I'm still on the job,
but I scream and shake.
I won! Just when
I'm drowning in disappointment
about my demotion,
the universe reminds me
I won't always be a waitress.

I have
    big things
            to do in the world.

5

It takes no time at all
for the doubts to crowd back in.
I start to think too much.

What will Dick think?
Will he recognize himself in Henry?
Will he get the message?
Do I want him to get
the message?

Will Smith take money
from my scholarship when
they see how much I won?

Will the contest open
new opportunities for me,
or will they realize
they picked the wrong person?

6

Today I chat with the other waitresses
for an hour or more.

They're all so pretty and sociable
and seem to love what they're doing.

I don't belong.

The feeling makes it hard
to relax or sleep or write.
The dark waters of
my ocean toss me
   up
      down
          sideways.
I thought this summer
would be different, but
I can't seem to get away
from myself.

My feet hurt.
No one asks me out for a date.
I'm probably an awful waitress.

I'm tired.
Lonely.
Scared.

I write Mother a letter.

I feel even worse.

7

Mother visits me at the hotel.

I'm not great company.
I can't stop feeling sorry for myself.
Every conversation leaves me
swallowing tears.

I didn't want her to come.
See me like this.
She has her own life,
so many burdens.
I don't want to be another one.

But when it's time for her to go,
instead of saying,
    "I'll be okay, Mother,"
I say, "Please will you come see me
on your next day off?"

I know.
I'm pathetic.

8

I consider quitting.
I've won five hundred dollars.
Wouldn't it be smarter
to spend my time writing?
But I've never been a quitter.

I tell myself I'm capable.
I tell myself, *You are not a coward.*
I tell myself, *You will not crawl back home.*

I stay.

9

Another week gone,
and I feel better.
My moods are confusing.
I must learn how to
deal with them.

I use my encounters for story ideas.
The characters around here are interesting,
almost to the point of preposterous.

Dick visits most evenings,
since he works nearby,
but I also date other men.
Gerald Brawner, a Princeton boy
visiting for the weekend,
takes me to an evening at
the Mill Hill Club.
I get all dressed up.
It's a delicious evening.
We dance and drink and laugh.

We make another date
to play tennis tomorrow.

10

Gerald shows up for our tennis date,
and I have a fever.
Another sinus infection.

"Can you drive me back
to Wellesley?" I say.
I'd rather be home than
stuck here when I'm sick.

He finds this hilarious.
But he agrees.
We spend the ride talking.
I'm sure the fever makes
my cheeks flushed and pretty.

He says, "Another time
on our date?"

I say, "Absolutely."

11

I'm in bed for a week.

Belmont calls.
They want to know if
I'm coming back to work.
Mother tells them no.

I hope this isn't
the start of another slide
into my ocean.

12

Friends send me "get well" cards,
and guess what arrives with them?
A letter from Harold Strauss,
Knopf's editor in chief.

It seems Cyrilly Abels,
the managing editor of *Mademoiselle*,
forwarded "Sunday at the Mintons' " to him.

He writes, "This struck me
as an extraordinarily deft
and mature story, far better
than the average
prize-winning story."

He hopes Knopf might publish
one of my novels someday.
He calls me gifted.
He says he expects
great things from me.

I write back immediately
and promise to keep in touch.

The universe keeps delivering.

13

For the first time in my life,
I find myself with
            days and days
of wide-open freedom.
I thought it would be refreshing.
   It's terrifying.

I don't know what to do.
How to keep myself busy.
How to manage these hours of
nothingness for the next
ten weeks.

It feels like I was some
industrious specimen,
rushing around in my
clockwork-like existence,
   accomplishing things,
     marking off tasks,
   enjoying myself in a way
I didn't have to think about,

and suddenly someone's lifted
      the bell jar
from around me and

the clock is gone and
I flail in an aimless reality
without any kind of purpose.

I fear this is the
   first step
into another
        dark depression.

I must find something to do.

14

I browse the classifieds
to find work. I consider
returning to the Cape.
I even miss Dick.
Or maybe I just miss activity.
Stasis leaves too much time
for thinking.
Ruminating.

I need to get out of Wellesley.
It's a suburban rut.

I stagnate.

15

I got a job!

I know I said
I'd never do it again,
after last summer's
horrendous experience,
but I'll work as a mother's helper.
Mrs. Cantor hires me
on the spot.

At least it will get me
out of Wellesley and
back on Cape Cod.

16

The Cantors are Christian Scientists.
They have three children:
    Billy, three;
    Susan, five; and
    Joan, thirteen.

They expect more from me
than the Mayos did.

I do dishes and laundry,
wash and wax the floors,
shop for food, polish their silver,
and help Mrs. Cantor cook.
And I look after the three children
at the same time.

But Joan is a teenager,
which makes things somewhat easier.
She often helps me clean up
while we listen to records
and dance.

And they're friendlier than the Mayos.
Mr. and Mrs. Cantor
invite me to talk to their dinner guests
after I put the children to bed.
We talk like old friends.
Mr. Cantor pays me extra
on those nights, too.
Like I'm the entertainment.
I don't mind.

They're so appreciative of my help
it makes all this seem like
fun, not work.

Since the Cantors live near
the Chatham Bars Inn,
I get to use their tennis courts
and private beaches. And they give me
loads of free time to do it.
It feels almost like
a vacation.

What a difference
from last summer's experience!

17

I meet Art Kramer on the beach.
He's intellectual
and wise and gentle.
He has a master's degree
in English! From Yale!
We talk about Joyce and Shelley
and Mann and Hemingway.
He brings me pieces from
The Atlantic and *The New Yorker*.
We talk about writing over lobster dinners,
and he knows what he's talking about.

He tells me about experiencing

anti-Semitism in Connecticut.
He was the only Jewish kid
in his school.
They beat him up.

He reminds me of Eddie.
It seems the two Jewish men in my life
are the only ones who take me seriously
and speak to me about literature
and politics and philosophy
as if I'm their intellectual equal.

That's worth something
in this world, isn't it?

18

Grammy and Grampy bring me
the August *Mademoiselle*,
with "Sunday at the Mintons'" in it.

I read it alone on the Brewster beach.
I can't help but giggle to myself,
dive into the sea and swim,
and return to the sand
to read it again.

It's wonderful to be alive
and full of
possibility.

19

I meet Val Gendron
at the Bookmobile that
stops in Chatham once a week.
I don't know how I'm lucky enough
to be there at the same time Val is.
She writes pulp fiction.
I bombard her with questions.

She gives me all sorts of advice.
She says, "If you have some
serious writing to show me,
I'll look over it and introduce you
to my New York agent."

I'm not sure anything is good enough,
but I go ahead and say, "Absolutely."

Val says, "Come by my shack."

We make a date.

20

Val doesn't live in a shack.
She lives in a red barn in South Dennis.
It looks like an artist's cave
on the inside.

She answers the door
in jeans stained with paint
and an old plaid shirt.
"I was doing my laundry
in the sink," she says.
She breezes out the door.
"Let me show you my yard."

She grows her own food
and makes her own jam
and dries her own herbs.
She serves me grapes, cake, and coffee.
She waves me up to
her second-floor workshop.
Every wall has bookshelves.
She has a desk with a typewriter
and stacks of manuscripts.
We sit in the middle of the floor
and drink our coffee and

pet the kittens who gather
around us.

It's cozy.

She lets me read some of her work.
She knows Rachel Carson and
went to school with
Ernest Hemingway's sister.

She slides me a *Writer's Handbook*
she got from the Bookmobile.
"This has all the big names," she says.
"And their addresses so you can
submit your stories and poetry."
It's a gold mine of submission opportunities.

"Wow," I say.

"Copy them down," she says.
"You'll need them, won't you?"

I copy about fifty of them.

Finally she says, "So.
Your writing?"

"It's probably not as perfect
as you're used to," I say.
"All kinds of things
wrong with it."

"Just hand it over," she says.
"You won a prize for it.
That's more than most people can say.
And that's your approval,
so don't apologize for your work."

It makes sense.
I give her "Sunday at the Mintons'."

We talk until midnight.
She drives me back to the Cantors'
in her old jalopy.
We have to yell at each other
over the noise of the engine.
She's my first hero.

21

I can't stop thinking about
how Val is so different from
Mrs. Prouty, my benefactress.

Both writers.
Complete opposites.

Which do I want to be?
Which will I become?

I can't be Val Gendron.
But I can take a good part of her
and make it a part of who I am.

I want to be me.

22

My emotions about writing swing
    back and forth,
  back and forth,
some self-made pendulum.
        One day
I'm in utter despair
over my lack of talent;
      the next
I'm on top of the world.

I'm in a good stretch now
as the summer winds down.

"Sunday at the Mintons'" published.
I've written a handful of good poems
since finishing my job with the Cantors.
I have a submissions list,
thanks to Val.

The only cloud in the sky is Dick.
He didn't get the message
in my short story.
For the remaining week in Wellesley
I eat almost every dinner with
him and his family, like
I'm already a Norton.

I must figure out
how to
escape.

The Most Important Thing in the World

Third Year at Smith, 1952-1953

1

There's not enough money
to continue staying
at Haven House.
I'll live at Lawrence House,
one of the cooperative dorms.
I'll waitress at lunchtime,
    don a uniform
to save two hundred fifty dollars
on room and board.

I only hope the extra work
doesn't send me crashing.

2

Lawrence House doesn't feel like home.
My roommate, Mary, decorates it
in bright yellows and aquas.
I manage to convince her

to change aqua to dark green
and suggest white curtains.

"It'll be more calming," I say.

She bites her lip.
I think she's going to argue,
but then she says, "All right."

I don't think we'll be friends.
She's a science major.
We hardly have
anything in common.

I miss Haven House.

Although I admit it's nice
being among people like me.
People who have to work hard
for what they have.
People who save
instead of spend.
People who understand,
    "I can't. I'm broke."

And it's diverse.
    Jewish students,

> Black students,
>   brown students.
It feels good to be part of it.

3

I meet Janet one evening
in the hall at Lawrence House.
We're soon fast friends, probably because
she wants to be a writer, too.

We're both taking the same
creative writing class.
We talk about books and
authors we love.

I keep other parts of my life
   my moods
   how I feel about Dick
   my worries for my future
private, though.

4

My English professors this term
are impressive.

Robert Gorham Davis has published
in *The New Yorker* and *The New York Times*.
Professor Patch is a literary genius
who loves Chaucer.
He teaches us in
his own personal library.
His bulldog, Jeeves,
joins us, sitting at
his master's feet
like an obedient pupil.

I feel stupider than Jeeves
around Professor Patch.
    Pitiful.
        Inadequate.
            Scared.

But I must succeed.
I can't give up.
I've begun making big plans
for after Smith:
    graduate school at Oxford or Cambridge
    a new life somewhere else
        studying and writing and
        making a name for myself
    escaping Dick and the
        pressure of marriage.

I don't have the money for greatness,
which means I have to
prove to my professors
I'm worth an investment.

5

There's nothing like seeing
your name in print.

I write stories for local newspapers
and the *Smith Review*.
It's especially gratifying
having a deadline,
doing the best you can
in the time you have,
turning in what you've got,
and seeing your article print
the next day.
    No long wait times.
        No almost-assured rejection.
    No obsessing over plot points
and character development.

This is real life.

I write stories for the papers
six days a week,
and it doesn't feel like work at all.
I could imagine a future
at a newspaper.

6

You know what feels like work?

Science.

Ten hours of science a week—
    ten hours!
Formulas, mind-numbing theories,
atoms, molecules, and
elements.

I don't understand it.
I hate it.
I want to drop it, but I can't.
It's required.
When will I use science
in my chosen profession?
I feel
    brainless,

    unintelligent,
        defeated
in this class.

Another of my stories,
    "The Perfect Setup,"
prints in *Seventeen*.

At least,
when all else fails,
I have writing.

7

More good news:
"Initiation" won third place
in *Seventeen*'s annual fiction contest
and will publish in January.

If I can keep up
these literary successes,
I might survive science.
And everything else.

8

A crack opens in my world.

Dick writes to say
he has tuberculosis.
He'll have to spend several months
at the New York State Hospital.

He writes, "Why is this happening?"
He writes, "Has happiness
    turned its back on us?"
He writes, "Come see me, Sivvy."

He expects everything to carry on,
almost the same as it always has.

How do I feel about it?
I can't say for sure.
I do know it will finally
give me the space I've needed
for a long, long time.

9

I had a chest X-ray done.
Mother advised it.

I don't have tuberculosis.

It's hard to contain the relief.
It's my twentieth birthday,
and this is a gift
that could just as easily
have turned into a curse.

Marcia and I celebrate
with sherry.

10

Mother brings me
a heart-shaped cake
for my birthday.
Ilo from my days at Lookout Farm
sends me an ink sketch.
I can't believe he remembered
my birthday.

I wonder if I should visit him.

My stomach flutters
when I consider what
we'd do on a visit.

11

Rodger Decker asks me
to the Princeton prom.
I say yes.

I wear my first pair of
high heels, black suede.
I feel chic and beautiful.

I shouldn't have wasted
money on them.

Rodger is intellectually stupid,
nothing more than a dumb rich boy.
I can't stand dumb rich boys.

I don't plan to ever
see him again.

It was nice to wear
those high heels, though.
I can't wear them around Dick,
because I'm too tall.

Every woman needs a pair
of high heels.

12

It's ridiculous to say,
      I know,
but I'm jealous of Dick.
All that time in a sanatorium
to read and write.
He's spending his days with
Hemingway and Yeats and
Faulkner and Salinger
and so many others.

What would it be like to have
so much free time at your disposal?
No classes that require careful study,
no job to steal your energy,
no expectations beyond your own.

What would I read?
What would I write?
Would I paint watercolors and
take music lessons and
fill notebooks?

"Don't you envy me?" he writes.

He doesn't know the half of it.

13

My studies swallow me.

I'm writing two papers for class
every week. I can't sleep.
I'm taking sleeping pills
just to close my eyes at night.
My head spins, constantly.

These girls are so smart.
Why do I feel the need
to keep up?
To surpass?
To prove I belong here, still?

I push myself to continue
constantly learning. Achieving.
Always.

14

My poem "Twelfth Night" will publish
in December's *Seventeen*,
and I can't seem to feel
anything about it.

I'm frozen.
Numb.

I don't know who I am.
   I don't know what I'm doing.
The rising tide of my ocean
spits my failures
out on the sand,
for all to see.

I have no control over
   my attitude,
     my feelings,
   my writing,
     my future,
   my hours,
     myself.
The center of my world

        collapses

no matter how
I beg it to hold.

I don't know how to live
in this blank hell.

15

I can't seem to tear my mind
from suicidal thoughts.

I think constantly of
Virginia Woolf and Sara Teasdale,
the way they ended their lives.
Is it destiny?
Does literary brilliance
require neuroses?
Will I go mad
or give up if
the constructs of society
and marriage and motherhood
stifle me creatively?

I tell myself
    I have everything!
    Girls want to be me!
    I should be bursting with joy!

It doesn't change anything.

I tell no one.

I put on my mask.
I pretend I'm happy and full,
not terrified and hollow.

Maybe my playacting
will knock me out of
my absurd self-pitying despair
and convince me to

       live.

16

I blame this wretched science class
for stealing my love of life.
I blame it for my declining
mental well-being.

I don't even want to
understand science.

It's stolen my will.
It's turned every small choice
into an overwhelming obstacle.
It's punched out
the center of my life.

I must escape it
or give in to
madness.

17

Eddie says I should talk to someone.
He sends me a list of
affordable clinics.

"This is serious," he writes.

He's right.

But help costs money.
I don't have money.

18

Eddie writes again.

He says I'm fully capable
of understanding science.
He says I've made the class
my scapegoat.
He says it represents
the way I feel about Dick—
right when I was going to end things,
he got sick with tuberculosis.

"And now you feel trapped," Eddie writes.

I don't answer his letter.

19

My English classes
keep me afloat.

Randall Jarrell,
   I. A. Richards,
      Edmund Wilson,
   Helen Gardner,
F. O. Matthiessen,
all masters in rhyme, metaphor,
   rhythm, sound, image.

I'm learning so much
I can feel my creative brain
ballooning.

Words are the most
important thing in the world.

They save lives.

20

Dick continues to send letters.
Now he fancies himself a writer.

Did he not once compare
a poem to a ball of dust?
Not even a ball.
A tiny little speck.

He sends me clunky poetry
and poorly plotted stories.
He writes a four-page analysis
of my work. He asks
if we should publish
our letters for
the literary world.

How tiresome
can a man get?

21

Irony is everywhere.

Dick, physically sick
but flourishing.

He feels his mind soaring.
He's free to do what he wants—
read or write or
sit in silence and solitude.

Me, physically well
   (but sick in other ways),
withering.
My mind is shackled.
I'm imprisoned by science
and assignments and
expectations I can't fulfill.

I send Dick bundles of books
I'd like to have time to read.
I don't mention my state.
I hide from everyone.

22

Thanksgiving in Wellesley
revives me a little.
Mother lets me loaf.
I absorb strength to live
through the next three weeks.
Until the next holiday.

I'm Lazarus,
    waking from the dead.
Embracing life anew.

23

I tell myself Myron Lotz
is more than a distraction.

I meet him at the Nortons'.
He's Perry's roommate at Yale.
The attraction is immediate.
He grins at me, shakes my hand,
and I'm in love.

Tall,
   handsome,
      and interesting.

His parents are immigrants.
His father works in the steel mines.
He's first in his class
and will graduate from Yale
a year early. He plans to start
Yale medical school next year.

I ask him to be my date
for the Lawrence House dance
on December 13.

He says yes.

24

I tell Dick that Myron's
my date for the dance.

He tells me, "Men who are
kind to you don't
make me feel jealous.
They make me feel grateful."

How ignorant
does he think
I am?

25

Myron spends the weekend
at Smith. We cruise
round the countryside

and take a long walk
up to the mental hospital.
"Want to go in?" I ask.
I'm curious about the people there.

He nods. "Sure."

The people inside scream and howl.
I'm both shaken and thrilled.

At what point
do people move from
sane to insane?
   How?
      And why?

26

I book an appointment with
Dr. Booth, the school physician.
I tell her I have insomnia.

"I stare at the ceiling
and try to turn off my brain,
but it doesn't work," I say.

"It races and flips and counts
and barks and shouts.
It's the loudest thing
in the room."

She doesn't say anything.

"And my science course," I say.
"It's killing me slowly."
I make sure to add, "Metaphorically."

She still doesn't say anything.

"I need to be free of it," I say.

That's all I tell her.
That's all she needs
to know.

"I can't do anything about
the course," she tells me.
But she gives me some pills.
"These should help
with the insomnia.
And sleep helps everything."

27

Christmas vacation is
a collection of obligatory visits—
>> the Cantors,
>> Mrs. Prouty,
>> the Nortons.

I used to enjoy
such whirlwinds.
Now they exhaust me.

28

I visit Dick over the holiday.
He can leave the hospital
for short excursions now
so we take a train
to Saranac Lake.
I can't bear the tension.

We can't kiss because of his illness.
I know it's awful, but I'm glad.
I don't have the courage
to end things, still.
I am spineless.

I drag him on and on.
We don't talk about the future.

That's just as well.

We visit Mount Pisgah to ski.
I've skied before, but
I'm still a beginner.

I plow face-first
into a snowdrift.
I laugh, get up, and
try to walk away.

Pain like I've never known
knifes through my leg.

My fibula is broken!

I telegram Mother.
"Not much pain," I say.
"But tricky to manipulate
while Charlestoning.
Anything to prolong vacation."

It feels like a message
from the universe.

Break free.
End things.

29

I get an A in my science course—
a higher mark than
my creative writing course,
which ended with an A minus.

How did I do so well
when the class almost
destroyed me?

What does it say
about the things that feel
          impossible?

30

Mother wants me to stay
at home and heal my leg.
But I need to get back to Smith.
I can't drown in sadness at home.
It'll be better at school,
with things to do.

She says she understands.
Maybe she does.

Still, I cry when she drops me off.
I can't help thinking
being shut in my room,
this cast limiting my movement,
will make me feel trapped.
Myron might lose interest
in a girl who can't walk.

But I'm really making
a big fuss over nothing.
The girls rally around me.
And I decide I will not
wallow in self-pity!
I will be cheerful and gay
and happy, and I'll tackle
my mental difficulties
the same way I attack
my physical ones:
            constructively.

31

A broken leg is
easier to overcome

than a broken mind.
I hope one's
journey to healing
will facilitate the other's.

Inactivity makes me feel
   tired
      uncomfortable
   disheartened.
But there is hope.

A garden grows
from a dead body.
Winter always turns to
spring.

Life begins again.

32

This semester will be
so much better than last.
I'm comfortable now at Lawrence House;
Dick is ill and can't come see me;
and I don't have to take
another damn science class!

I have Myron.
I love my new classes.
I've left my burdens behind.

I'm healthier.
I'm happier.

I have a broken leg,
but loveliness is on its way.
I can feel it.

I write papers,
exercise like it keeps me alive,
read *The New Yorker* and
     study
          study
     study.

I'm applying for a guest editor spot
at *Mademoiselle* this summer. If I get it,
I'll spend a whole month in Manhattan.

What a dream that would be!

33

I don't believe
everything happens
for a reason.
But it does some good
to find a little purpose
in the bad.

Is it terribly naive to say
my broken leg has expanded
my social circle?
I've come to like Mary,
and the other women
in Lawrence House seem friendlier.

Good comes with bad.
Life is a series of battles
between the two.

34

Eddie's not convinced
by my boisterous mood.

"I'm genuinely looking forward
to spring," I write him.

"My leg will be healed, I'll bike again,
the fields will be alive with
green and hope!"

He says, "You're tossing bouquets
to distract yourself.
You need to see a psychiatrist.
You promised me."

He thinks I broke my leg
deliberately.

Really, he can be
the most ridiculous person
who says the most ridiculous things.

I tear up every reply and tell myself
he doesn't deserve one.

35

Dick writes.
He's down in the dumps
about how long
his recovery will take.
Ten more months.

"It's intolerable,
not being together," he writes.

If only I could say the same.

36

I don't want to marry Dick,
but I could certainly imagine
marrying Myron—
    or someone like him.
I could build a creative life with him—
I could face the world with him—
    or someone like him.

He asks me to the
Yale prom in March.
Of course I say yes.
I try to tame my enthusiasm,
but it practically spills out of me.

"I want to look gorgeous," I tell the girls.

"You will," Mary says.

The next six weeks

I'll live in the rapturous bliss
of anticipation.

37

After Theodore Greene's lecture
on "Protestantism in an
Age of Uncertainty,"
I come back to the house
and Mary says, "There's a man
waiting for you in the parlor."

I dash upstairs to change into
a red sweater and skirt,
much more attractive than
what I was wearing.
I'm fully expecting to see Myron,
on a surprise visit,
but instead I see the most
   handsome,
      tall,
   brown-haired boy.

"Hello, Sylvia!" he says.

His name is Gordon Lameyer.
He's an English major,

a senior at Amherst.
His mom told him to call on me
after she met me at
Wellesley's Smith club.

We have practically
everything in common.
    Wellesley kids,
        Unitarians,
    German fathers.
And we love literature.

He asks me out.
Myron's gone maddeningly silent
since he asked me to Yale's prom,
    so I say yes.
Gordon smiles and pushes
a lock of curly hair behind his ear.

He's a dream.

How strange, the way
the universe works.
It drops a lovely English major
from the sky just when
I need him most.

38

Gordon and I spend
our first date in his
Amherst room,
discussing James Joyce.
"I'm a Joyce fanatic," he says.

"Oh!" I say.
"I'm thinking about writing
my senior thesis on *Ulysses*."

He's delighted.
The fire crackles.

Is there anything better
than sitting by firelight
with a handsome young man,
discussing Joyce?

39

Myron sends me a postcard.
I ask him to Rally Day.

The only thing better than
one brilliant, handsome man

showing interest is
two.

40

I write off February
as the Black Month.

Myron cancels our weekend plans.
Gordon's busy and can't come visit.
I'll spend my first
cast-free weekend alone.

The doctor lifts my cast off
like a coffin lid.
He says my leg
hasn't completely healed.
It looks repulsive,
    withered and yellow
  and embarrassingly full of hair.
I take a razor to it,
so no more hair,
but it also takes some skin.
My ankle's still swollen
and green.

I'm rotten.
My leg proves it.

41

I distract myself with poetry.
I write three villanelles
and send them to *The Atlantic*
and *The New Yorker*.

I think I'm getting better,
   word by word,
      line by line.
At least *something* improves.

Life is tedious and
insufferable just now.
But I won't cry.
I'll write villanelles instead.

42

I finally write Dick
the letter I should have sent
ages ago.

"I'm seeing someone
else," I tell him.
"I'm not sure I want to marry.
I want to pursue a career."

I don't tell him
I don't want to marry *him*.
I should have.

He writes back.
"I'm so lonely here," he says.
"Death frightens me.
I don't know if I want to
be a doctor anymore.
I feel depressed and stagnant,
and I can't write anything creative.
My only light is you.
Don't say you don't want to marry.
We'll make it through this."

I can't help thinking it's pathetic.
He sounds so desperate.
I don't want to wound him more.
I feel terrible about it all.

But why should I feel terrible?

He's created the perfect image of
    Sylvia Plath
during our separation.
    Real Sylvia
can't possibly compare to
    Sanatorium Sylvia.

43

Perry's engaged.
She's a Middlebury student.
They haven't known
each other for long.

I can't help wondering:
Is he the one
who got away?

44

Dick urges me to waitress
at Lake Placid this summer,
so I'm closer to him. The Nortons
pressure me for the same.
They have no right to

insert themselves into
my future plans.
Maybe I should tell them
he's not a virgin so
they won't think me so heartless,
breaking their perfect son's heart.

I have no intention of
waitressing at Lake Placid.
I plan to work for *Mademoiselle*
or take some classes at
Harvard Summer School.

I control me.

45

Myron takes me
to the Yale junior prom.

I wear a strapless
silver-lavender dress.
I get my hair cut—
    the popular pageboy style.
I look quite glamorous.

We have a splendid time.

We spend most of our
weekends together after that,
driving around Vermont
and reading.

I let myself
fall in love again—
       no pressure for marriage.

I like it best that way.

46

The New Yorker sends me
a handwritten rejection
of my poems.
I got so close!

I try again, send them
more of my villanelles.

Seventeen publishes
"The Suitcases are Packed Again"
and accepts "Sonnet to a Dissembling Spring."
It doesn't feel like much anymore.

I've set my sights
on greater accomplishments.

47

W. H. Auden is teaching
at Smith this spring!
I heard him speak for
the first time today.
He even looks like the perfect poet—
tall with a yellow mane of hair
and the kind of voice
you could listen to for hours.

48

Warren's snagged himself
a Harvard scholarship.
His news gives me confidence
to apply for a scholarship
at Harvard Summer School.
I'd like to take a psychology course
and a creative writing course
with Frank O'Connor.
It'll give me something to do
if I don't get the internship
at *Mademoiselle*.

49

My modern poetry seminar
brings me to life.

We study Eliot, Yeats,
Dylan Thomas, Wallace Stevens,
Marianne Moore,
and of course Auden.
I love Eliot's *Four Quartets*.

This class makes me certain
I'll stick with creative writing.
No more psychology or
journalism or philosophy.

I was born for
          this.

50

I've been elected
to Phi Beta Kappa,
and I also learned I'll be
the *Smith Review* editor
next year.

It's the one job on campus
I really wanted!

The universe is smiling
on me again.

51

I finally muster up enough
courage to ask Auden to dinner
at Lawrence House.
Some other English majors join us.

Picture us circled around
the wooden dining hall table,
hanging on every word
that falls from his mouth.

That's what it should have been.
    Instead,
we don't even talk about poetry!
He talks about current events
and ordinary things.

After dinner, we continue
the trite conversation in
the living room.

I try to ask him
about Wallace Stevens.
He asks us if we've
ever been on blind dates.

What?

Well, he's still
the most brilliant man
I've ever met.

52

Auden visits my evening
modern poetry seminar,
which gathers in Ms. Drew's
living room. He reads
one of his poems, and
we analyze it for two hours.
He talks about art and life
and poetry and the sea.
It's much better than
our dinner the other night.

The evening was
the joy of my lifetime, I think.

I plan to show him
some of my poems.
I must.

When will I get
an opportunity like this
again?

53

I show Auden
one of my poems.

I shouldn't have shown him
one of my poems.

Enid comes with me.
"You'll be discovered," she whispers,
right before we walk
into his office.

I hand Auden my poem.
It's the best one,
out of all I've written this year.
And he's not impressed.
He doesn't have

a single good word to say.
He has only criticism.

"You should watch out
for your verbs," he says.
"This is superficial,
     overemotional,
   melodramatic.
A little over the top."

His criticism is
a little over the top.

I want to forget.
I will never forget.

Who do I think I am?

54

Harper's accepts "Doomsday"
   The hour is crowed in lunatic thirteens
and "To Eva Descending the Stair"
   Clocks cry: stillness is a lie, my dear;
and "Go Get the Goodly Squab"
   Hide, hide, in the warm port
   Lest the water drag you to drown.

They're paying me
one hundred dollars!

Harper's is the real deal—
I'm on my way!

Next up: *The Atlantic* and
The New Yorker.

I telegram Mother
with the news
for her birthday.
"It's all thanks to you," I write.
"The best person in my world."
Mother likes to hear
things like that.
She doesn't have to know
I don't completely mean it.

I tell her nothing of Auden
and his criticism.
But I will say:
    it feels a little like
        I've proved him wrong.

55

I make it into
Mademoiselle's final round
of guest editor assignments.
It buoys me. I have so many
class papers to write—
      fifty pages' worth at least!—
before May 20.
The deadline is
breathing down my neck,
but at least this is
a good bit of news.
If I get it, maybe I can afford to
live at Harvard while
going to summer school
for the last part of the break.

My dream summer
is falling into place.

56

I go on a shopping spree
and spend nearly all

my *Harper's* money on
    the most divine black silk dress
        with a matching jacket,
    a pinstriped suit dress in navy and white,
    a pair of white linen French heels,
    and a brown patterned dress.
All very practical, sleek, and stylish.

I may not have
a place to live this summer,
but my clothes are professional.

I'm an author now.
No more common clothes!

57

I write Dick about a stimulating weekend
I spent with another man.
I want to be honest with him.

Apparently, it was bad timing.
He'd just come out of surgery
and was recovering
when he got my letter.

His mother writes to chastise me.

"He doesn't ever complain
about his bleak days," she says.
"But if there's any kind of justice
in his life, he'll live
the rest of his happy
and fulfilled."

I try to let her words go.
Her son isn't perfect.

But then Perry lets it slip
in a letter that his mother
doesn't want me to marry her
"precious, courageous" boy anymore.
She thinks I'm selfish because
I'm not by Dick's side
every moment I get.
She thinks I should be
helping Mother financially,
not going to Harvard Summer School.

What business is that of hers?
I'm not her daughter.
And I don't want her life.

When I think of
how close I came
to stepping into that
backstabbing judgment,
    marrying Dick,
I quake.

58

Mother's having
ulcer trouble again.

I tell Warren he should
support himself and
not lean on Mother so much.

I want to earn enough
so she doesn't have to
ever work another summer.

"We have to prove to her
that we're happy, successful,
and independent," I write him.
"Even if it's just an illusion."

Warren says he understands.
We'll see.

59

I know I'm a hypocrite.

The same day I write
all that to Warren
I have to write Mother:

> PLEASE PUT A GOODLY
> SUM OF MONEY
> IN MY CHECKING ACCOUNT
> AS SOON AS POSSIBLE
> AS I AM DOWN TO
> ONE DOLLAR.

I add,

> "One hundred dollars
> would not be amiss."

60

I got it!

One of the twenty guest editorships
at *Mademoiselle*!

I feel like a fairy godmother
just granted my biggest wish!

I'll be working five days a week
starting June first, and I'll earn
one hundred fifty dollars
minus room and board.
I'll stay at the Barbizon Hotel.
Only women are allowed
to room there.

I'll finish at the end of June
and will have a week to recuperate
before Harvard Summer School.

Here comes my future!

61

Professor Davis sends us
off into the summer
with some grand advice.

He says, "I hope none of you
plan to be writers.

Women writers are
frequently unhappy."

He's our creative writing professor.
He teaches only women.
Why the hell would he say
something like that?

God, it must be nice to be a man.
To have so many options
    (and opinions).
To be given an opportunity
to achieve literary greatness.
To fulfill artistic ambitions,
    judgment-free.

To be taken seriously.

What do I have to do
to be taken seriously?

The Bell Jar

Summer 1953

1

I am equal parts
   nervous,
      excited,
   and thoroughly terrified.

A *Mademoiselle* guest editor!
Only twenty students
get it every year!
Women hardly ever have
a chance at internships
in the literary world,
and this is one of them.

I still can't believe
I got a spot.

I will prove myself this summer.
I will be the hardest-working,

most talented writer
they have on staff.

2

Before setting off
for New York City,
I brush up on the history
of *Mademoiselle*.
Here's what I know:

Founded in 1935
At the time it was the only
American magazine published
for women eighteen to thirty years old
with above-average education

Seventy-nine percent
of its readership
    (half a million readers)
has attended college or
graduated with a degree

Women hold almost all
the senior staff positions there

It publishes a "Jobs and Forums" column
for career girls

Writers like Katherine Anne Porter,
Auden, and Carson McCullers
have published in it

How could I *not* belong here?

3

I make it to Grand Central Station.

Two muscular soldiers
shoulder my bags and
hail me a taxi.
They accompany me all the way
to the hotel on the corner of
Sixty-Third Street and Lexington Avenue.
I feel almost like royalty.

The Barbizon is magnificent.
Seven hundred rooms!
Twenty-three stories!

It's the color of coral,
with royal-looking columns
and no sharp edges.
It has a library,
    a swimming pool,
        recital rooms,
    squash courts,
a sundeck,
    a solarium,
        and a formal dining room.

When you walk in,
you just get a feeling:
        This is where
        the young women
        who will make
        something of themselves
        collect.

Only women are allowed
past the ground floor.
We even have a curfew!

The staircase is delightful.
You look over the railing
of a mezzanine and can see
everything and everyone below.

It's grander than any place
I've ever known.
And I get to live here
for a month!

The woman at the front desk
points me to an elevator.
She says, "The bellhop
will help you get to the right floor,"
and nods toward the next guest.

I'd be content to live in the elevator—
it's larger than my bedroom at home!
The ride is so smooth
I can hardly feel it moving.
So I ask the bellhop, "Can I ride
up and down a few times?"
I don't care if it makes me look childish.

He smiles and says,
"Whatever you'd like, miss."

I ride to the top
and back down
five times!

4

My room is on the fifteenth floor,
number 1511. It has green carpet
and a dark green bedspread.
The walls are beige.
It's very chic.

They've given us a dresser,
a desk, a phone, a radio,
and a sink. We use
communal bathrooms
at the end of the hall.

The only downside
is there's no air-conditioning.
You'd think a fancy place like this
would have it.

I leave my windows open all night,
and the city sings me to sleep.

The blaring horns of cars
are a sweet music in the morning.

All the activity of this city
feels productive.

5

My first day begins with
an unfortunate nosebleed.

I'm all dressed up in my new suit,
and the blood stains my blouse.
So I change into
my brown patterned dress
and worry the whole way to
575 Madison Avenue
that it doesn't look
professional enough.

Turns out I don't have the time
or the need to worry.

I spend the morning meeting editors.
One is Carson McCullers's sister,
Rita Smith.

Betsy Talbot Blackwell,
the editor in chief of *Mademoiselle*,
introduces us all and gives us our schedules.
First on the agenda: a short coffee break.
There's a lot of talking and laughing

on the elevator down to the lobby,
probably to defuse the tension we all feel.

We don't want to mess this up.

6

After our coffee break,
I share an elevator back up
with a girl named Neva.
Our conversation strays to
Blackwell and other editors.

"They're certainly
a motley crew," I say.

"Betsy Talbot Blackwell could be
an Irish washerwoman, with her
pale skin and freckled arms," Neva says.

The girls behind us snicker.
Neva's eyes get wide.
We've been talking like we're alone.
None of these girls are our friends.
Neva isn't my friend,
and I'm not hers.

It's only a matter of time
before someone tells Blackwell.

7

Blackwell calls Neva and me
to her office.

She rips into us.

"How ungrateful you must be,
to say such unkind things
about the editors you work for," she says,
her face red and sweaty.
She points a finger at Neva.
"I didn't want you here
from the beginning."
She turns to me. "And you."
She looks me up and down.
"The only reason you won a spot
was because your mother has
sent us so many stellar secretaries.
I bet your mother took care
of a lot of things, didn't she?
Maybe even your assignments?"

I'm so shaken I can't say a thing,
not even to vindicate myself.
I feel hollow and so angry
I can hardly see straight.

She dismisses us.
I'm completely numb
as I walk out of the office.

Neva and I immediately
run to a bathroom and sob.

I suppose we're friends now.

8

I will show
Betsy Talbot Blackwell
who I am.

I will work harder than any other
guest editor this summer.
I will prove she doesn't
know me at all.
That my mother didn't
lift a finger to help me

with my assignments.
That I deserve to be here
on my own merit,
not because my mother
knows how to train secretaries.

I hate her,
but I will
prove her wrong.

9

Someone calls Neva and me
out of the bathroom.
It's time for a photo shoot.
The magazine wants to do
a "Jobiographies" feature.

We compose ourselves
and follow the rest of the girls
to the studio.

The photographer asks each of us
what we want to do in our future and
hands us props that supposedly
symbolize our ambitions
and career choices.

"A poet," I tell him.

He looks at me twice,
then hands me a rose and
points to a sofa with
a bowl of fruit beside it.
"Sit there," he says.

What ridiculous,
patronizing nonsense.

    "Come on,
  give us a smile,"
he says.
I smile, but I turn
the rose upside down.

Click.

We'll see
who has
the last laugh.

10

Blackwell and Cyrilly Abels
    the *Mademoiselle* managing editor

join me and two others for lunch
at the Drake Hotel.
I'm on edge the whole time.
I keep thinking of Blackwell's words.
The only reason you won a spot
was because your mother has
sent us so many stellar secretaries.
She couldn't dismiss me,
but she probably wanted to.

Everything I do feels wrong.

Maybe I made
a mistake, coming here.
It's hard not to see this
disastrous first day as an omen.

The lunch itself is thrilling, though.
We sit in a dark room,
    sip sherry,
        eat chef's salads,
    discuss writers and magazines
and exciting things.

I keep my mouth shut.
I don't want to be remembered
for what I say.
I want to be remembered
for what I do.

11

Our editors tell us not to forget
   the hats and gloves,
   silks and fancy evening gowns
we packed
when we're out and about.
We have an image to uphold.
We're classy *Mademoiselle* interns.

We're supposed to
avoid the "jazzy" places and
stick to the more affluent ones.
We'll dance at the St. Regis Hotel
or the Plaza, not one of
the "lower" places.
They even dictate where we dine—
only at preapproved
Upper East Side restaurants.

I feel like I'm suffocating.
I don't belong here.

An evening gown?
How does one afford such a luxury?
After room and board and tipping
     cabbies ten percent
     waiters fifteen percent

what will be left of the
one hundred fifty dollars
they'll pay me for the four weeks?

Hamburger Heaven's
the cheapest restaurant,
but it's still steep—
    fifty-five cents for a hamburger!

The magazine won't
pay our taxi fare for
events or appointments.

Looks like I'll be eating
Hamburger Heaven and
walking everywhere.

12

My second day is much
more successful than my first.

I attend a fashion show
at a fancy hotel.
The clothes are lavish and superb.
We lunch at an oyster bar.

I get a makeover at a
salon on Fifth Avenue.
I keep my hair mostly the same,
but it feels good to preen a little.
Still myself, but more sophisticated.

I've almost put
my horrid first day
behind me.

13

Later that afternoon we meet
in the magazine's conference room,
all the guest editors dressed alike:
    penny loafers, white blouses
       buttoned to the top,
  long wool skirts, and beanies.

They want a group photo of us.
They cavort us out to
Central Park for hours.
We look absurd.
And it's much too hot.
The photographer keeps making us

move and shift, trying to
shape us into the perfect star.

I get to write copy for the picture.
I settle on, "We're stargazers this season,
bewitched by an atmosphere
of evening blue. Foremost
in the fashion constellation,
we spot *Mademoiselle*'s own tartan,
the astronomic versatility of sweaters,
and men, men, men—we've even taken
the shirts off their backs."

It's fun writing,
but I'd rather write something
that matters.

14

I know I'm lucky to be here.
So many girls would kill
to be in my place:
    Guest Managing Editor!
One of the highest positions!
It's an honor!
I even get to interview

Elizabeth Bowen,
    one of my heroes,
for a short piece on
women writers!

But I can't help thinking
I would have made
a good guest fiction editor.
Why couldn't I have been
chosen for that?

I should be grateful for the opportunity,
but instead I feel terribly disappointed.

Blackwell probably knows that.
It's why she's singled me out.
It's why she dislikes me so.

I should be content.
The problem is
       I've always wanted more.

15

At least I get to read some manuscripts
along with all the other copy

I have to manage.
I've seen work from
>   Dylan Thomas,
>   Elizabeth Bowen,
>   Noël Coward.

I record my comments on them.
I even sign some rejection slips—
one today for a man on
the *New Yorker* staff.
I feel a sense of poetic justice.

I tell myself
all this is making me
a better writer.

But I'd still rather be
writing my own stories.

16

Cyrilly Abels is brilliant.
A little scary, but brilliant.
She keeps a box of tissues
on her desk for

the girls she makes cry.
There are so many of them.

I try not to be one.

We share an office.
I work at a card table in the corner.
She gives me assignments,
and I try to do them to perfection.
I have to read all the copy
and manage deadlines.
I say please, thank you,
try to be polite.
I compliment her endlessly.

She's tough on me.
She makes me go back
and do things again.
She rarely has a good word to say.
She pushes me hard.

It's overwhelming,
but I keep at it, because
it's what I do.
    It's what I must do.
        It's who I am.
I tell her I can do what she asks,

and I write and rewrite and
rewrite again until I'm
    sick sick sick
of words that mean
nothing in the end.

17

On the weekend I'm free.

I visit the Museum of Modern Art.
An exhibit on postwar Europe
draws me in. It's distressing—
    famine, death,
        prisoners of war, destroyed lands.
I can only look for so long
before I have to turn away.

Laurie, another guest editor,
meets me at Washington Square Park,
where an art fair is going on.
It's lovely.

I hear all kinds of languages
when I walk the streets.

And on Sunday we visit
Central Park and the zoo.
The caged animals remind me
of the beggars who ride the subway,
and once that gets in my head,
we have to leave.

I don't know if I'd call it
a good weekend.

18

I spend all week writing,
talking about, and editing
pieces on sweaters.
    So versatile!
       So lovely!
    So can't do without!

It's all drivel. I need to
write something of substance.
Read something of substance.
Do something of substance.

This city is too much for me.
Life is hard and fast here.
I don't know who I am in it all.

I want to be on the Cape
writing my stories.

I must get into Frank O'Connor's
creative writing class at Harvard.
It's my only way out of fashion
and consumerism and capitalism
and a city that never sleeps
even though it should.

19

Elizabeth Bowen writes to
congratulate me for what she calls
"a brilliant start"
to my career.

I don't know how she can say that.
My story about women writers,
the reason I interviewed her,
got slashed by my editors.
One paragraph is all
Elizabeth Bowen got.
It was a footnote.

It was too important
to be a footnote.

"Send me more of
your writing," she says.
But I'm afraid I'll only
disappoint her.

20

I want to have grand
experiences in New York
so I can write about them,
but I can't afford them.
I need to find a man,
      or more than one,
who can take me out,
foot the bill.

The magazine's guest editor dance
at the St. Regis Hotel provides
the perfect opportunity.

The hotel sets a magical scene,
everything rinsed in a rose glow.
We watch the sunset on the rooftop
with cocktails in our hands.
Two live bands play.
A photographer freezes us
in time.

He catches me
in a glamorous pose
   smiling,
   holding a daiquiri.
I know I sparkle.

But even as that thought
crosses my mind, another one
cancels it out: *This isn't me.*
It's someone else.

All the men here
are educated, accomplished,
rising stars trying to
make their mark on New York.
They were invited by *Mademoiselle*,
as if our editors didn't trust us
to bring our own dates.

This is an edited life.

Three men try to steal my attention.
The best-looking one asks me
on a beach date next weekend.

Yes. Please get me
out of here.

21

I have to cancel the beach date.
It's raining.

But I'm almost relieved.
I've been working and
socializing nonstop.
I need a break.
I walk Manhattan alone
and draw buildings and people,
things I might later use
in my writing.
I make the most of
my solo pursuit.

My money's nearly gone.
Mother paid for my hotel bill,
because I needed money to eat.
I had to miss Warren's graduation
from Exeter because
I couldn't pay for the bus fare.

This place swallows money whole.

22

I've added a few experiences
to my third week here:

A Yankees game and
seeing the interior workings
of two other magazines:
Living for Young Homemakers
    (I understand what they're trying to do,
    but young women aren't just
    homemakers anymore)
and *Charm*.
The guest editors attend a luncheon
at an advertising agency,
where they have my favorite foods:
      crabmeat and avocado salad.
I confess I eat more than what is
socially acceptable for young ladies.
People look at me askance.
I try not to care.

I regret it, though.

Something must have been
wrong with the food.

I start vomiting on the ride home,
and I think I'm never going to stop.

We all vomit. We spend
nearly all night in the bathroom.
In the morning the hotel doctor
sticks us with needles and
pumps fluid back into our veins.
Some of the girls
feel better after that,
but I stay in bed the rest of the day.

It's the most awful kind of agony.
Dying would be a mercy.

23

The ad agency sends gift baskets
with Hemingway books and fruit.
As if that would make us forget
our miserable experience!

Poisoning is bad advertising
for an advertising agency.
Can we even trust the fruit?

It's what they do, though.
Rot our minds.
Make us doubt ourselves
    and our worth.
Make us believe we lack something
so we spend our dollars
chasing beauty or fashion or
whatever fills the hole and
makes them money.

Our sickness is
a metaphor.

24

I try to be grateful for my time here,
but all that matters in this
    shiny, glittery world
is sex and money.

We're programmed to be
objects for men to observe
and admire and lust after.
That's what fashion's for.

I'm not an object.
I'm a subject.

The subject of
my own life.

Everyone here is selling something.
Everything comes with a price.
New York fashion is flashy and colorful
    and empty.
There is nothing
intellectual about it.

I hate it.
I want to leave.
I want to quit.

I have to stay.
It's the worst sort of torture.

My world is
imploding.

25

This morning I read about
the imminent execution
of the Rosenbergs.

Life is a tragedy.

No one seems
particularly bothered that
the Rosenbergs will be executed.
No one seems to see
the injustice of it—
    that they're innocent,
        that the only reason they'll die
    is because they're Jewish.

I try to engage with Neva at breakfast.
She eats a Danish.
I can't eat anything.

"Everything okay?" she says.

My only answer is to shove
the newspaper in her direction.
"The only reason they're killing them
is because they're Jewish."

She says nothing.
I feel disgusted by her indifference.
I probably do a terrible job hiding it.

I walk to work with Laurie.
We pass a newspaper stand,

and she says she's fine with
the Rosenberg execution.

Why does no one else
find this a hideous violation
of human rights?

Miriam, another guest editor, is Jewish.
She should care.
She doesn't.

They're all dreaming about lingerie
and the perfect skirt and
what hairstyles are "in"
for the next season.
Who are these people
surrounding me?

26

My last week at *Mademoiselle*
kicks off in a blur.
Blackwell hosts a farewell party
in honor of us,
and we see George Bernard Shaw's play
   Misalliance

at the Barrymore Theatre
and we tour
    Macy's and the *Herald Tribune*.
I try to stay strong
to the finish.

But I'm sinking
           fast.

27

This whole *Mademoiselle* experience
was supposed to be the
high point of my year,
and instead I wrote drivel,
    met callous men,
        posed at fashion shoots
all dolled up.
I did absolutely
nothing of consequence.

I didn't even get to meet
my literary heroes who
regularly write for *Mademoiselle*—
    Truman Capote,
    Dylan Thomas,
    Tennessee Williams.

Dylan Thomas is the one
I regret the most.
Every time he visited
I was out chasing
some flimsy story that
I could write in my sleep.

I've let everyone down,
including myself.
I'm not sure
how to live with that.

I write to Mother:
"I will let you know
what train my coffin
will come in on."

I want to think I'm jesting.

I'm not sure I am.

28

I offer Neva
some of my clothes
on our last day.

"I'll take some of yours
if you take some of mine," Neva says.

I don't want her clothes.
But I smile a plastic smile
and say, "Deal."

That night Neva and I ride
the elevator to the roof.
We toss our waist-cinchers
and girdles into the wind.
We throw out the pieces meant to
restrain us.
    Imprison us.
        Steal our freedom.

We laugh the whole time
we toss our bindings.

29

Laurie invites me to her room.
"Take anything you like," she says.

I take a green skirt
and a white peasant blouse.

The outfit is too young for me.
I take it because I'm tired of fashion.
I'm tired of dressing the way
someone says I should dress.
I'm tired of all the gowns
I'll never be able to afford
and hearing them called
the latest looks.

I may never take
this childish ensemble off.

30

Mother and Grammy
can't hide their shock
when they meet me
at the train station.
I know what they see:
    hollow eyes
    a child's dress
    my ocean swallowing me.

I can't even manage to
pretend everything is fine.

Everything isn't fine.

New York has crushed me.

After asking about
the internship and
hearing my monotone answers,
Mother looks uncomfortable.
At first I think it's because her
    chatty Sivvy
is holed up inside
this silent, vacant one,
but it turns out she's trying
to figure out how to deliver
more bad news.

"I got word that
Frank O'Connor's
creative writing class
is full," she says.

Why am I not surprised?
The universe knocks you down,
and it likes to kick you
while you're there.
You're an easy target.
Everybody loves easy targets.

My stomach wrenches.
"So I didn't get in."
   Voice flat,
      no emotion,
   but storms inside
are roiling and shaking.

"You'll have to wait until
next summer to register," Mother says.
She eyes me from the rearview mirror.
I stare out the window.
Her eyes feel like torches
scorching my face.

I don't tell her I won't apply
next summer or any other summer.
I already submitted my best work,
and it wasn't
        good enough.

I may never write again.

31

I can't stop thinking about
Harvard Summer School.

I think this rejection
is the universe's way
of telling me it was cruel
to so obviously base
the character of Henry
    in "Sunday at the Mintons'"
on Dick.
A moral oversight.
Reprehensible.

Maybe I should take
a course in psychology,
instead of writing.

I can't take another
course, though.
It costs too much,
and I need money for my
senior year at Smith.

32

I've decided to stay home
for the rest of the summer
and learn shorthand from Mother.
I'll write. I'll get a head start
on my James Joyce thesis.

If Smith threatens to lower
my scholarship because
I'm not working, I'll tell them
I slaved away at *Mademoiselle*
and learned shorthand for
the rest of the summer.
It's a more logical thing to do.
They can't fault me.

The only problem is that
last summer, while at home,
      the bell jar
lifted, nearly breaking me
with its wide-open freedom.

But
    the bell jar
is not what I thought it was then:
routinized, productive, safe.
Really,
    the bell jar
sucks all the life out of a person.
It oppresses. It imprisons.

    The bell jar
is still here this summer.

But now I can feel it
closing
  down
    around
      me.

33

What am I doing?

I keep hearing Mrs. Norton's
scathing criticism in my head.
  Spoiled,
    over-protected,
  selfish.
  You wanted time to write,
  and now that you have it
  you're paralyzed.
    You haven't written a thing.

I try to distract myself
by visiting Gordon Lameyer
every day until he leaves
for Rhode Island in mid-July.
I picnic with Marcia.
I play tennis.

I survive,
but it can hardly be called
living.

34

Gordon and I walk
along the beach and talk.

I wish we didn't talk about
the great poets.

"You know, all the great poets
have been men," Gordon says.

I'm so shocked I can't speak.
He continues. "Men create art,
women create people."

I have never been so
     hurt
     furious
     hopeless
in my life.

35

Fear swallows me whole:
        I will never be great.

I didn't get into
a creative writing class
because I'm not a
      good enough writer.
Maybe I should quit.
But writing is the only thing
that brings me joy
in this life.

I can't eat.
I feel sick and tired
and anxious and troubled.
I have dreams and fantasize
about ending it all—
    with a razor or pills
        or some method that's foolproof.
I see myself locked up
in a hospital, a drain
to my family.

Maybe this is
the beginning of
the end.

36

Mother tries to teach me shorthand
for an hour every morning.

I can't seem to get it.
Her instruction blurs
into another language.

We last four days.

37

I stripe my legs with razors.
I cover up the wounds,
but Mother notices.

"I just wanted to see
if I had the guts," I say.

Mother grabs my hand.
"The guts for what?"

She's trying to keep calm,
but her voice pitches up
like a wail.

I want to laugh it off.
But my voice matches her wail.
"This world is wretched!
    I don't want to live anymore!
        Come die with me!"

Mother calls our family doctor.
I should have known
she'd get a doctor involved.

Next time I'll remember
to keep my mouth shut.

38

I see Dr. Racioppi today.
She refers me to another physician.

My problems
    it seems
require more expertise
than a family doctor has.
They require a psychiatrist.

39

Mother convinces me to
volunteer at Newton-Wellesley Hospital.
I'll be a nurse's aide.
She says it will help me
think less about myself,
focus on helping others.

It's certainly
a different environment.
But not necessarily healing.

I feed dying patients.
I see death everywhere—
    old women, babies,
        young people.
It's awful.

I hate sickness.
I feel too much
for their suffering.

What's worse is knowing them.
My old art teacher,
    Miss Hazelton,
is here.

Mother thinks
this is my cure
for self-pity.

I can't help but think
it's my punishment.
    My coffin.

My end.

40

Mother says, "I think you need
to relax, Sivvy. Rest.
Stop putting so much
pressure on yourself."

I sunbathe with a book.
But I don't read.
I can't read.
The letters scramble and run away.
My brain can't decode them.
I finally tell Mother, "I can't read."

"What do you mean,
you can't read?" she says.

She won't understand.
I say, "I have no goal."

"Of course you have a goal."

She won't understand.
I say, "I can't read, I can't write,
what will I do with my life?"

Mother blinks.
She opens her mouth.
She closes it again.

No one
has an answer
for me.

That's not true.
There is one who has
an answer for me.

His name is

        Death.

41

Mother takes me to see
Dr. Thornton
    my psychiatrist
in Boston.
He's ghastly,
overconfident and arrogant.

He reminds me of Dick.

I can't talk to him.
Or maybe I won't.

42

Another appointment
with Dr. Thornton.

He tells Mother
I need shock treatments.

He would not have dared
recommend shock treatments
after two sessions if I was a man.

I know what they do to women.
I know what's at stake here.

I can't sleep
    because of him.
I feel even more anxious
    because of him.
I will not recover—
    because of him.

Why couldn't Mother have
found me a woman doctor?

I know the answer.
Most of them are men.
They consider ambitious,
strong-willed women abnormal.
We are defects. We're hysterical.
We make big deals about nothing.
We're too emotional. They put us
in hospitals and don't let us out
until we're ready to resume
our proper roles—
    cook, clean, care for children, shop,
        just be a woman already.

We return home and
are promptly recommitted
if we cannot commit
to the life permitted us.

They believe
    our sanity
is tied to
    our domestic capabilities.

43

Mother consents
to the shock treatments.

I may never be the same.

44

We drive to Valley Head Hospital
in Carlisle.

It looks innocent enough,
walking in. But I know
I've come here to die.

They lead me to the shock unit.
They arrange electrodes on my temples.
Those electrodes will blast
my brain with an electric current
so I'll seize up—
     which is why they
        buckle me down with a strap
        that dents my forehead.
They give me a wire to bite
so I don't mangle my tongue.

They hope my electrocution
will repair my brain
and cure my anguish.

The silence is excruciating.
I close my eyes.

And then something
jolts me so violently
I think my bones might snap.
Blue and white sparks
flash across my closed eyelids.
My insides fly out.
There is nothing left.

But they say all is well.
Patients sometimes break
their backs getting shock
treatments, they tell me.
I'm one of the lucky ones.

I was electrocuted.
I woke up alone.

But I was one of
        the lucky ones,
because I'm still able
to walk myself
   out of the room.

45

No one talks to me after the treatment.
They give me sleeping pills.
My brain is utterly fried.

46

They wheel me down to the room.
They electrocute me again.
They murder me.

Over and
   over and
      over again.
I do it because I don't want
to be institutionalized.
The doctor has all the power.
The patriarchal medical establishment
has all the power.
They found me neurotic
for my passion and ambition,
for my iron will.
They want to shock it out of me,
but it is all of me.

What will be
left of me
when they're done?

47

At home my thesis
on James Joyce's *Ulysses*
is the only pleasure I have left.

Ms. Drew set me up well.
I have all my notes

from her literature class.
I've made all the
symbolic connections.
    Identified motifs.
        Uncovered themes.

But I can't understand any of it.

I try to read Joyce's words—
        they're nonsense.
I try to read my own words about Joyce—
        incomprehensible.
    I don't recognize letters,
  words slide right by,
it's all some strange language
of symbols and shapes.

I'll never pull this off.
I thought I could be
a woman who defied tradition,
who laughed in the face
of the tiny little boxes society
folds around us. But I can't even
understand James Joyce.

Why did I ever think
I was made to be great?
I will fade away like
the billions of women
before me, hardly noticed.

Maybe they'll say
   I knew someone once
      who tried to be something
   she was not.
   I can't recall her name,
      or any of the drivel she wrote.

Maybe I will be
   a footnote in history.
Maybe I won't even be that.

Who can say what dreams die?
Who can say whether we die
with them?

48

Joyce said, "When the soul of a man
is born in this country
there are nets flung at it
to hold it back from flight."

I want to fly.

But there are
  so
    many
      nets.

49

Marcia comes to see me.
We go to the beach.

"Let's swim out
to the raft," she says.

It looks so far away.

"It's only a few feet
from shore," she says.

I'm too tired,
but I do it anyway.
I'm still trying to offer the world
the illusion that everything is fine.

I sit on the raft,
staring at my legs
dangling in the water,
almost disappearing at the feet.

"Sivvy," Marcia says.
"Are you okay?"

Words spill out.
"Do you know the truth, Marcia?"
Of course she doesn't.

She shakes her head.

"I have sat in my room
with my paper, and my mind
is a massive blank."

Marcia says nothing.
I'm probably scaring her,
but I can't stop. The words
rocket out of me. "I'm blank.
People think I have this
great writing power and that
the images just pour out of me
and the fact is my mind is blank."

Marcia wraps her arms around me.
"I can't sleep," I mumble
into her shoulder. "I'm afraid.
I don't know if I can
ever go back to the way
I was before."

She says nothing.

Cries for help
are never loud enough.

50

Another shock treatment.

More bits of me fly out
and splatter the room's walls.
It's torture.

Mother has scheduled two more.
I can't endure two more.

What if it goes on
forever?

I'll make a clean end of it.
It will be better for
my family in the long run.
It will certainly cost less.
And they won't have to
watch me waste away
in a sanitorium.

I'll spare us all.

51

    I play a part.
  Pretend.
Convince everyone around me
that I'm not dead inside.

People are so absorbed
in their own lives.
They don't even notice.
They make it so easy.

I visit Cambridge,
   play tennis,
      go to parties,
  visit Marcia,

      dance at the Totem Pole Ballroom,
    lounge on the beach,
        eat with the Cantors.

I see the doctor.
    Survive my electrocution.
Then join friends for dinner.

Sylvia is well.
Sylvia is okay.
Don't worry about

        Sylvia.

52

Mother's going to see a play.
I act like I'm thrilled for her.
Really, I'm thrilled
at the opportunity,
left at home with
Grammy and Grampy.

"I don't want to
leave you," Mother says.
Warren's at work. She's worried

Grammy and Grampy won't watch me.
I'm counting on it.

"You deserve the time off," I say.
"I'll be fine. Don't worry."

I'm so convincing, she goes.
Grammy and Grampy
recline in the backyard.

No one watches me
break Mother's safe and
steal the sleeping pills
Dr. Tillotson prescribed.

I write a note.

"Went for a long walk.
Will be home in a day or two."
I prop the note on a bowl
of flowers Mother keeps
on the table.
It looks almost cheerful.

I hide in the basement crawl space,
stacking a pile of firewood

so no one will see me
if they look down here.

I swallow pill after pill.

No telling how many
before the blissful dark
sweeps me into
blankness.

53

Flashing lights,
    voices everywhere,
        pricks and prods.
Is this a nightmare?

No. This is real,
and one thing is for certain:

        I'm alive.

"Oh no."

I think I said
the words out loud.

Warren and Mother
and Grammy and Grampy
won't let me die.
The doctors won't let me die.
They all drag me back into
my hellish, meaningless
existence.

"I love you," Mother says.
She has tears in her voice.
I can't look at her face.
"We all do. We are so happy
you're still here."

I am not happy I'm still here.
What I did was
my last act of love.
Don't they know that?

54

Eight days at Newton-Wellesley.
I'm sure this is costing Mother a fortune.
And what about what happens next?
The doctors will lock me up.

I know it.
How will Mother pay for it?

My family will have no money
because of me.
They'll lose the house
because of me.
They'll be destitute and hungry
because of me.

I've ruined everything.
Why couldn't they just
let me die?

55

This is the most expensive
illness I could have.
I wanted to spare Mother that.
It hurtled toward me.
I got tired of sidestepping,
so I tried to hurtle back.

Mother tells me, "Mrs. Prouty
will take care of everything."
She'll pay for my stay

at the mental hospital.
She has money enough.

"You don't have to worry
anymore, Sivvy," Mother says.
"You just need to get well."

I suppose it's time to try.

56

Letters come.
Ms. Drew calls me
the best English student
at Smith, by far.
She says I don't even
have to work at it—
     I just am.
She says she thinks
my breakdown is
a symptom of burnout.
I pushed myself too hard.

Evelyn Page,
   another Smith instructor,
writes and apologizes
for not talking more with me

about the difficulties
and strains of writing.

They both tell me they wrestle
with depression.

Another professor says
plenty of creative people
have been through something
like this, and they always
come out stronger.

"Your teachers all want you
back at Smith," Mother says.
"They hope you'll graduate."

What do I want?
Everything and
nothing.

57

Gordon writes:
"You're the greatest girl
I've ever known.
You were made for extraordinary things.
Never forget that."

"Get well," he says.
"You haven't failed
anyone," he says.
"We all love you.
You make life worthwhile."

But words feel
      meaningless
sometimes.

58

It's strange how crises show you
your important people.

Who steps up to say,
    "We love you anyway."
Who extends a hand and says,
    "I will help you back up,
  just lean on me."

Who sticks around.

59

Dick's detached tone

in the letter he sends
is a studied example
of severance.

"Sivvy, I can sympathize
with your status as a patient.
I sincerely hope you
recover quickly."

He's probably rejoicing
that he never officially asked me
to marry him.

Neither of us will
come out and say it.
We'll just go our separate ways.
Breakup understood.

60

The biggest challenge
is yet to come.

I have to rearrange my life,
make another comeback,
get to work again.

The hope of it
makes me want to recover.
I work hard at it.
I do everything I'm told.

I want to see my friends,
    to love my family,
        to appreciate everything I've done
    and everything about the world,
to chase my dreams again—
           that's what I'm working for.
I have to believe it's still possible.

Life After Death

McLean Hospital and Recovery, 1953-1954

1

Mrs. Prouty arranges my transfer
from Massachusetts General Hospital
to McLean Hospital. It's supposedly
the best mental hospital in the country.

I ride in a limousine,
courtesy of Mrs. Prouty.
The building reminds me of Smith,
which soothes my nerves.
The grounds look like a country club.

But no matter how pretty
it is on the outside,
inside it's just a place
where broken people go.
And nothing will erase
the fact that I am one of them.

2

Dr. Beuscher is my new idol.

She's young,
   intelligent,
      wears stylish clothes,
and has big ambitions.

Her husband also works as
a McLean psychiatrist.
From the outside, they have
the perfect partnership.
They both work in the same field,
and probably have
so much to talk about.

My mind is open and ready.

3

Mrs. Prouty sends me
one of her manuscripts to type.

It feels so similar to writing
I can almost convince myself
the words are mine.

I ask her to send me more.

4

Mother brings me yellow roses
for my twenty-first birthday.

I throw them away.

I admit to Dr. Beuscher
that I'm angry with Mother.
    All her expectations,
        all her hovering,
    all her dashed dreams
and cheerful "You'll beat this, Sivvy."

Dr. Beuscher suspends
Mother's visiting hours.

It feels thrilling
to have such power.

5

They've suspended
my privileges, too.

They say I'm retreating
into myself again.
Now I can't leave McLean
for drives with Mrs. Prouty
or walk the grounds alone.
They censor my mail.
I wander up and down the halls,
with no purpose or destination.
I need something to do.
It doesn't even have to be
something complicated,
just a distraction.
How does anyone live
without purpose?

I don't feel like
I'm getting better.

6

The doctors transfer me
to another ward.
They prescribe Thorazine.

I feel lethargic and lifeless
on medication.

I'm trapped in a world of
    powerlessness,
  inactivity,
pointless existence.

7

I knew it wouldn't be long
before they tried to kill me.
And now they'll do it
from the inside out.

Dr. Beuscher said
I wouldn't have to endure
electroshock treatment again,
but the other doctors
lay out their plan:
    Six treatments.
  And no guarantee
I won't have more.

I refuse to do it.
I won't let them kill me
from the inside out.

But I have no power here.
So once again they electrocute me.

8

I can now have visitors
and leave for drives with Mrs. Prouty
and take supervised walks.
Nothing is unsupervised.
Someone is always watching,
even when I walk the halls
inside the hospital.

I can't remain
a
    prisoner
        forever.

9

Jane Anderson from Smith
is also a patient here.

We have a strange,
competitive relationship.
It's like we're trying to see
who will be cured first.

She believes in psychotherapy.
I think it's all nonsense.

Somehow, she's winning.

10

The days start to look a little brighter.

I meet the McLean librarian.
She's a Smith graduate.
We talk about all sorts of things—
   Smith, writing, great books.
I hole up in the hospital's coffee shop
and sketch and write letters.

Mr. Crockett,
   my old English teacher,
visits me once a week.
I play card games
with the other girls.
Gordon writes faithfully.

I think this might be
the way up.

11

I write Eddie.

"Here I socialize with
concert pianists and
brainy scientists from MIT.
The patients come from
Cornell, Vassar, Radcliffe.
It's like a country club."

What I don't say:
I'm still a prisoner.

12

Dr. Beuscher prescribes me
a diaphragm.
She says, "Every woman
should be free to explore
her sexuality."

What an interesting world this is,
at least when run
by women.

13

I'm now allowed
to leave McLean
on weekends.

Phil McCurdy invites me
to Harvard. We spend
the day browsing bookstores
and shops in Harvard Square
and dance the night away
at the Totem Pole.
On the drive back to Wellesley,
he stops on a dark, empty street
and we neck in the car.

I think
I'm coming back
to myself.

14

I spend Christmas with
Mother and Warren and
Grammy and Grampy.
I reread all of Gordon's letters
he sent me at McLean.
I write him a letter on
Warren's new typewriter.
"I'm feeling one hundred
percent better now," I say.

For Christmas, he sends me
a book of Edmund Wilson essays.
I have high hopes that it will
remind me how much
I loved Yeats and Joyce and Eliot.
I have high hopes I'll be able to
understand what I read.

15

I spend every weekend at home.
I'm still a McLean patient,
but I'm slowly earning
my freedom.

The doctors are letting me
return to Smith.
I'll be late for the semester,
but my professors say
that won't be a problem.

They only agree to my return
because I promise to see
the Smith psychiatrist
twice a week
and cut back on how many
courses I take.

There is life after death.

16

Dr. Beuscher advises me
to take a few years or several
to decide what I'll do with my life
and who I'll marry. If I marry.
"All the important
life decisions," she says.
"Take your time."

Her words ease a pressure
I've carried for years now.

I ask her about sex.
    What should I expect,
    does it hurt,
    does it complicate things.

"I know I prescribed a diaphragm," she says.
"But don't get sexually involved for now.
You're too fragile to handle
all the emotions involved."

I try not to take offense.

"But that won't be true
forever," she adds.

17

Dr. Beuscher pulls me
into her office to
say goodbye on my last day.

I tell her, "You've been
like a mother, except
without all the
disadvantages."

She looks pleased.
She even pinks a little.

She doesn't say anything except,
"I'll truly miss our time
together, Sylvia."

We All Wrestle Demons

Fourth Year at Smith, 1954

1

I beg Warren to drive me
back to Smith.

"Why don't you ask
Mother?" he says.
"I'm sure she'd be happy
to take you."

Isn't *he* happy to take me?
He doesn't understand
why I'm angry with Mother.
And truthfully, I don't, either.

"I don't want her there," I say.
"It's too much pressure."

"She only wants what's
best for you, Sivvy."

"Easy for you to say.
You don't have to be perfect."

"You don't have to
be perfect, either."

I don't try to explain the
pressure I feel from Mother.
Warren drives me back to Smith.

And on our way,
we hit a blizzard!
Warren tries to get up a hill
and we slip and slide and spin
and the seconds and minutes
stretch out in slow motion.

We're going to die, I think.
*The universe is going to
take me anyway,
after all this work.*

Several more seconds of spinning pass.
I think, *This can't happen to us.
It was supposed to go differently.
I'm supposed to be great!*

And just like that,
the car finally skids
to
    a
        stop.

Warren and I are so relieved,
we can't stop laughing.

2

I have my own room now.
The girls shuffled around
so I could be alone.
I decorate the room with
    gray curtains,
    a maroon coverlet,
    blue pillows, and
    some of my favorite wall prints.
I bring in two bookcases
and fill them with books.

I spin in my room.
I am home.

3

Mrs. Kelsey is the new
Lawrence House mother.
The girls and I have tea in her room.
They're all very smart
and lovely.

My schedule is manageable,
much lighter than it's ever been.

Nineteenth-Century Intellectual European History
Early American Lit, 1830–1900
Russian Lit

I'm auditing Modern American Literature
and Medieval Art.

Before class I work
in the Lawrence House kitchen
chopping vegetables,
which is preferable
to waiting tables.

I'm trying on a new attitude:
    "There's no such thing as perfect."

4

It does me good
to be back in the world
of learning.

I play whatever part
suits the situation.
I wear masks and laugh loud
and live large—anything
to make them forget
what I did over the summer.
Today I'll be the cultured creator,
    tonight I'll be the tantalizing temptress,
        tomorrow I'll be the coffee-shop girl
    who writes in all the spare spaces.

Next week, who knows?
Lady or tiger?

5

No one mentions the summer.
All my worries and fears
melt away. It's like
nothing happened at all.

I don't want to dwell
on the past.

Still, the shadow chases me.

I try to live each day
as fully as I can.

6

I lose friends,
gain others.

I'm a different person now.
It's what happens.
    You grow,
        you experience,
    you split apart
and leave some behind.

I count among my confidantes:
    Marcia
    Nancy
    Pat
    Jane
    Claiborne.
We don't talk about

our dreams or ambitions
or deep things at all.
It's safer.

7

I want to experience
all of life.

Little things, large things,
I want to do much more
than I've done:

Bike and hike through Europe.
Travel out west.
Meet people I want to know forever.

I want to
     see everything
     hear everything
     know everything
there is to know.

I want so much more
for myself.

8

I don't like Dr. Booth
as much as I like Dr. Beuscher.
We speak philosophically, mostly.
She's not even a psychiatrist.
She's a professor of public health
and bacteriology.

But I have friends
I confide in now.
I have no problems to speak of.

I am well.

9

Cyrilly Abels invites me
to New York City for lunch
during my spring break.
Since I want to face the demons
that broke me last summer,
I agree.

I plan to stay with Ilo Pill.
Who cares if it makes people talk?

This is my life to live.
We'll have a great time, I'm sure.

I'll face the city
the way *I* choose
this time.

10

I visit Warren and his friends at Harvard
for the first weekend of spring break.
They're delightful.

I meet Dr. Beuscher for coffee.
We talk for hours.
I consider her one of
my best friends now.
She's only nine years older
than I am. That's not
too large a gap for friendship.

When I tell her about
my New York plans, she says,
"I think that will be
very good for you."

11

I meet Cyrilly at the Drake Hotel.
We don't mention my summer at *Mademoiselle*
or my mental hospital stay.
It's just as well.
I don't want to talk about it.
We mostly discuss authors
she knows personally,
like Dylan Thomas.

"He'd drink on an empty
stomach," Cyrilly says.
"All the time. Great amounts."

We all wrestle demons, I suppose.

12

On my way back to Boston
I stop off to meet
Sarah-Elizabeth Rodger Moore
in Connecticut.

Clem, Warren's roommate,
set up the meeting.

She's his mother, and
she's a writer.

She shows me her mansion.
Her study alone is spectacular,
with a view of the trees and lakes,
and more books than you can count,
in bookshelves along the walls.
Her typewriter sits in
the center of it all.

If I had a room like this,
I'd write all sorts of remarkable things.

Someday, I will be
penning my fiction and poetry
in a dream house
    in a dream office
        in a dream part of the world.

13

Phil McCurdy takes me
to a cabaret dance at Harvard.
A cute boy,

Scotty Campbell,
asks me to dance.

He's the assistant director
of Harvard Summer School.

"I thought about applying," I say.
"But I'm undecided. I was rejected
last summer."

"You?" he says. "Rejected?"

He's probably trying to be charming.
He whirls me round the floor.

"You should apply again," he says.

"I don't know. Maybe."

"They could never reject
a brilliant girl like you."
He has a hundred more compliments.

But they did reject me.
I don't know if I want to
get my hopes up only to

have them crash again.

I think he'll forget me.
But he sends me a letter
that practically promises
a spot and a scholarship if I apply.

So I do.

Some might say it's not right,
the way it came about.
    Dancing,
        flirting,
    paying attention to a man
with power.

But I know
   that's how
      you play
         the game.

14

I write my first poem in a year.
It's quite good, I think.
Maybe even excellent.

I like it so much
I write another.

15

I've left behind my need
to make perfect grades.
When you come as close to dying
as I have, your priorities shift.
You start to understand
   what matters and
      what doesn't.
You live with
   a different purpose.

Who will ask about
my specific grades
in the future?

No one.

16

I have one dollar left
in my bank account
when some good news comes.

Smith awards me an almost full scholarship:
    one thousand, two hundred fifty dollars
    donated by Olive Higgins Prouty.
I'll only have to make up
three hundred dollars
for my senior year.

It's the biggest scholarship
Smith has ever given.

Is it because of my stay
in a state hospital or because
    I am Sylvia Plath?

17

I dream of escape.

From Mother and her hovering,
    American womanhood,
        American men.

I want to spend a year in Europe.

The fantasy takes hold.

18

I'm considering applying
to Oxford or Cambridge as
a Fulbright fellow—
or going to graduate school
at Columbia or Radcliffe.
Maybe I'll join the
Women's Naval Reserve
so they can foot the bill
for my higher education
and I can travel and
see the world and
collect experiences
for my fiction and poetry.

I'll write about it all.

19

Final exams are looming.
I study ten hours every day.
My joints stiffen from
leaning over my desk,
my brain won't shut down at night,
and my body is in desperate need
of physical exercise.

At least I can still study.
Electroshock treatments didn't steal
my intellect and creativity.
It's a relief.

20

The semester ends
with a bang.

I'm pretty sure I ace my final
in Early American Lit.

Alpha Kappa Psi,
    the college arts society,
elects me president.

And my poem "Doom of Exiles"
wins the Ethel Olin Corbin Prize.

I treat myself to a blond bob
to celebrate my rise
from the grave.

Casting Off

Summer 1954

1

Harvard Summer School
awards me a full scholarship.

I'm deliriously happy
I won't have to spend
another summer serving food.

How different
this summer will be.

2

Mother rents a cottage on the Cape.
Nancy comes to visit.
She's never seen the sea!

We take long walks along Nauset Beach
and go see Mrs. Prouty and
eat cucumber sandwiches

until we're queasy. We double-date
with Phil McCurdy and
Norman Shapiro, his tutor,
who's studying French poetry.

We're regular girls
with regular appetites,
and I can almost imagine
we live with no expectations
on our heads.

3

Marcia marries Mike.
I drink too much
at the wedding.
I only remember
good-looking men and
boisterous conversation, before
Claiborne helps me home and
puts me to bed.

I try to apologize to Marcia
in the morning,
but she won't have it.
"I'm worried about
you, Sivvy," she says.

"Don't worry about
me," I say. "I'm the
same old Sivvy."

She doesn't believe me,
but I pretend not to notice.

4

I don't go to Claiborne's wedding.
Two other friends marry,
and I skip their weddings, too.

Don't they know
there's plenty of time
for settling down?

They've made their choice.
I'm standing by mine.

5

I decide I need to see Dick
and clear the air.

He seems to have shrunk,
both in physical stature

and personality.
What did I see in him
all those years ago?

"I'm sorry for leaving things
the way I did," I say.

"I think it was for
the best," Dick says.
And that's all we say about it.

We swim. I tour the infirmary.
He loans me his bike
for the rest of the week.

And then I leave,
relief and pity
braided tight.

6

For the summer I live
in a one-bedroom apartment
a block from Harvard Square,

along with three roommates:
   Nancy,
   Joan, and
   Kay.

Joan and Kay are fellow Smith girls
from Lawrence House.
They sleep on a sofa bed
in the dining room. Nancy and I
share the bedroom, in exchange for
being the resident cooks.

I'm taking Elementary German
and Frank O'Connor's
Nineteenth-Century Novel class.
I'm excited to see how
Professor O'Connor will
open my mind in
luminous new ways.

Nancy and I spend our first week
in Cambridge exploring and
meeting boys for drinks and coffee.

A promising start.

7

I get to meet Richard Wilbur!
His mother-in-law lives in Wellesley
and knows Mother.

I feel nervous and
don't talk as much as
I would have liked.
I've read every word he ever wrote.
I want to tell him he's brilliant,
but I can hardly speak in his presence.

I'm not sure
I make the impression
I intended.

8

I study hard for my German class.
I feel like a failure when
I earn a B on the exam.
My father was German!
Shouldn't his language
come naturally?

I probably shouldn't have
taken the class. All those
magnificent writers,
forgotten on my shelf
so I could study German.
And for what?

At least Professor O'Connor's class
makes this an intellectually
stimulating summer.

9

Ira Scott, a Harvard professor,
takes me out.
We eat steak and talk
by candlelight.
We have a lovely time.

"I'm married," he says.

I shrug and hold up my drink.
"Cheers."

10

I spend nearly every day with Ira.
We go on long walks
and drink daiquiris and
talk over more steak dinners.

On August 24,
    the anniversary of my suicide attempt,
we sail in Marblehead.
He makes me forget
everything wrong in my world.

When we return to the apartment,
Nancy tells me Mother called
while I was out.
"She was frantic," Nancy says.

"I was shopping," I say.
Which isn't true, but
Nancy doesn't need to know.

"I couldn't find you," Nancy says.
"Your mother was worried."

I call Mother. "I'm fine," I say.

She says, "I want you
to see Dr. Beuscher."

She never has to tell me twice.

I take a sedative to help me
get through the rest of a cursed day.

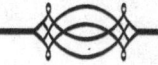

The Highest Vocation

Last Year at Smith, 1954–1955

1

My first days back at Smith
are consumed with applications:
    Fulbright Fellowship,
    Woodrow Wilson Fellowship,
    Radcliffe, Cambridge, Oxford.

I gather
    three health exams,
    twelve statements of purpose,
    twelve letters of recommendation.
Mary Ellen Chase,
    George Gibian,
      Alfred Kazin,
    Newton Arvin, and
Elizabeth Drew give me
fantastic recommendations.
None of them mention
my suicide attempt or
my time at McLean.

Someone told me Oxford
and Cambridge aren't welcoming
to lady suicides, so I'm hoping
my professors have enough prestige
and renown to overshadow
my hospital record.

But just in case,
I also ask Dr. Beuscher
to write a recommendation.
She can assure them
I'm healthy and fit and
ready to take on grad school.

I hope it will be enough.

2

I still work as a waitress
to fund my stay at Lawrence House.
This year I have breakfast shifts,
but at least it will force me
into bed early.
Less than eight hours of sleep
    I've learned
can trigger a downslide.

I'm determined to make
this year my best.

It's a light load this semester:
    Miss Dunn's magnificent Shakespeare class,
    Alfred Kazin's short story writing course,
    intermediate German,
       which will be horrendously hard.
I can barely stammer a sentence
in the language.

But best of all is my Dostoevsky thesis.
I spend all my free time on it—
    reading,
       writing,
    analyzing.

It invigorates me.

3

I join the Lawrence House
crew team. We practice
three days a week.

Exercise keeps me
healthy.

We row on the water,
and I feel peace.

4

Alfred Kazin is brilliant.

He says discipline is
as important as talent.
He says it's our duty
to write every day.
He doesn't want me to bother
with his class assignments
but has freed me to work
on my own,
with the agreement that
I'll turn in lots of compositions.

I'm going to write
more than I ever have
this year.

This is
the beginning of
my dream.

5

I meet Ellie in Kazin's class.
We immediately connect.
She has so much
in common with me.

We talk of Yeats and
Russian literature and
writing and acting.

I tell her about McLean,
my shock treatments,
my madness.
The nightmares.
The fear that it will
happen again.

Her brother disappeared
from Dartmouth earlier this year.
Her family hasn't found him.

"I understand the pain
of losing someone
you love," she says.

Maybe that's what

draws us together.
Or maybe I just
need a friend.

6

Several of my poems
publish in *Harper's*.
I win some contests.
Cyrilly Abels buys
    "Love Is a Parallax,"
for *Mademoiselle*,
and I get an A minus in German.

I fly.

Have I ever been this
happy in my life?

The light is made brighter
by the dark.

7

Alfred Fisher has taken me on
as his private poetry student.

He wants me to help him
research John Ford,
an Elizabethan poet
and playwright.
He also wants me to turn in
some poems every week.

He's helping me build
the discipline of writing.

I know that every time
one faces a blank page,
there is a flash of horror.

>   *What will I write?*
>   *Will it be any good?*
>   *Who do I think I am?*

I think we conquer it
with practice.

8

Five days back at Smith
after Christmas and
I already have a

    sore throat,
    cough, and
    congestion.
I rest, but I also write—
five new poems I send
to *The New Yorker*.

Peter Davison comes to visit.
He says Mr. Kazin sent him.
He's impressive—Harvard degree,
Fulbright at Cambridge.
His British father is a poet.
And he's an assistant editor
at a major publisher,
      Harcourt, Brace.

He asks to see
any novel I might write.

What a pleasant surprise.
This world is certainly
a strange, remarkable place.

9

I still live with a voice.
It screams,

"Traitor!

Faker!

Imposter!"

It's terribly hard to tolerate.

Maybe we all live with a voice.
What does yours say?

10

I thought I would need
some revisions on my thesis,
but my professor calls it
a masterpiece!
I send it to the typist
almost a month
ahead of schedule.

It looks beautifully professional.
I'm not sure I've ever been
prouder of something I did.

I skip class to proofread
its seventy pages.

It really is a masterpiece.
They better make space for me
in the literary world—
          because I'm coming.

11

After January exams I stay
in Wellesley for a rest.
I take advantage of
a short midwinter break.
I sit around in pajamas,
    play piano for hours,
        and sleep.

I see Dr. Beuscher,
and we talk about religion,
philosophy, a woman's career.

And, on a good note,
Mother and I are
getting along.

12

I have a full load this last semester:

three English classes!
    The Twentieth-Century
    American Novel with Kazin.
       An English review unit
       with Evelyn Page.
    A poetry tutorial
    with Alfred Fisher.

Fisher has me writing
more poetry than I
ever have before.
My typewriter is hardly ever still!
The poems keep coming.
Nine new ones in
the first two weeks.

I think I'll collect them
into a volume to publish.

13

The interview for the
Woodrow Wilson
graduate fellowship is grueling.
I sit across from four smug men,
including the Harvard dean,

and try to answer their
barrage of questions.
Why are they all men?
Couldn't they find any
intelligent women to include?

They ask me if I will,
    in the future,
forfeit my career for marriage.
Will I have babies?
    Will I marry a teacher?
How do I plan to keep
    writing and teaching
with a home to run?
    How will I do it all?

They don't ask men
these questions.

I have to pretend
their line of thinking
doesn't bother me or infuriate me.

It's the worst interview
I've ever had.
I feel like a criminal

standing before a firing squad,
four rifles pointed at me.

Why do men have
such power?

14

I don't get the
Woodrow Wilson Fellowship.
I figured this would happen.
I'd already tempered
my expectations.

The firing squad made up their minds
about me before I even
walked in the room—

        because I'm a woman.

I shouldn't be surprised
anymore.

15

All I seem able to write

is self-gazing drivel about
whether or not I have
what it takes to make it
in this world.

I don't know if I do.

The fellowship interview
broke something in me again.
I know I shouldn't let it.
But they're terribly smart men—
and I'm a woman with
an asylum stay in my past.
What could I possibly
offer the world?

I keep writing, though.
It's all I can do.

16

I worry I won't get into
Radcliffe because of the
Woodrow Wilson Fellowship.
But the dean writes to assure me
that's not the case.

"The fellowship is given
mostly to men who want to study
law or medicine or business," he says.

While terribly unfair,
I'm relieved to know
my rejection was not because of
my character blots or
my stay at McLean.

17

I interview for a
one-year teaching position
in Tangier, Morocco,
at the American School.

It would be a great opportunity.

But when I tell Mother,
she says it would be better
to take teaching classes
or learn shorthand.
Rage explodes in me.

Shorthand? The only thing

I want to do is write!
It's my whole delight in life!
I refuse to trade what time
I'd use to write so I can learn
shorthand and type someone else's
manuscripts and poems!

When will Mother understand
that she doesn't get to
steer my life?
I write my own future.

18

Columbia writes to say
they've appointed me
a graduate residence scholar.
I'll have free room and board
and they'll cover five hundred dollars
of my tuition.

I could go to Columbia for free,
since Smith gave me
a one-thousand-dollar
graduate fellowship.
I might even have money

left over.

But all I can think about
is going to England.
Newnham College in Cambridge
accepted me, and I'm in
the final round for the Fulbright.

What if I get it?

I know it's a gamble,
but I turn down Columbia's offer.

19

I'm a finalist for the
Glascock Poetry Prize.

I join the five other finalists
at Mount Holyoke College,
where we enjoy
a whirlwind of celebrity.
First I have lunch with one of the judges,
    Marianne Moore.
She's like an incognito
fairy godmother.

We get interviewed on the radio
and have our photos taken for
   Mademoiselle and
   The Christian Science Monitor
and then it's time for
our readings at the college.
My poems sound polished
and the audience laughs
in all the right places and
applauds in all the right places,
and it makes me supremely happy.

The spotlight suits me.

I tie for first with a boy
from Wesleyan.
I get fifty dollars.

20

The Atlantic is publishing
"Circus in Three Rings."
They want me to change the title, call it
   "The Lion Tamer" or
   "The Tamer"
and revise my first and last stanzas.

I'm not sure how I feel about it.
Poetry is more complicated
than prose. If you butcher
a poem too much,
it may not sing.

I talk it over with Alfred Fisher.

"It's up to you," he says.
"You're the poet. But sometimes…"
He pauses. "You could try it
and see how it goes."

I try it and see how it goes.
And I send the revised version
back to the editor—
not because it's better
but because it's the only way
they'll print it.

I also include five other poems—
maybe the editor will pick one of them
instead of "Circus in Three Rings"
and my poem will remain
    whole
instead of
    butchered.

21

I drop my German class.

I tell myself it's not an insult
to my father's legacy.
One only has so much time
and capacity to learn,
and I want to focus on
literature and poetry.

I think my father
would understand.

22

It's a month full of honors:
Another Ethel Olin Corbin Prize
Clara French Prize for being the top senior in English
Marjorie Hope Nicolson Prize for my senior thesis
Radcliffe acceptance
Academy of American Poets Prize
Honorable mention in the *Vogue* Prix de Paris

I've earned four hundred sixty-five dollars

from writing and prizes
this year!

23

I win a Fulbright Fellowship
to Cambridge.

I call Mother at
Newton-Wellesley Hospital.
She's there because of her ulcer again.
I hope the news will help ease her worry.
I celebrate with friends.

The world is mine,
and I will take it.

24

I survive finals and will graduate
summa cum laude.

Mother arrives at my graduation
on a stretcher mattress, because
she just had stomach surgery.

I told her to stay home,
but she said, "I can't miss
your graduation!"

Kazin and his wife
blow me kisses from the audience.
Mary Ellen Chase tells me
to reach out if I run out of funds
in England.

Adlai Stevenson speaks
at our commencement.
He tells us we should strive to be
good housewives and mothers
and support our husbands
wholeheartedly.

As if I came to college for that.

I'll do so much more.
My highest vocation
is not marriage,
it's writing.
    It's my first love.
        It has all of me.

After the ceremony
Mother, Grammy, Grampy, and I
have a picnic at Quabbin Reservoir.

It's a wonderful send-off.

A New Life

Summer 1955

1

I spend the summer after graduation
in Wellesley, doing
everything I love—
   writing,
      reading,
   wandering.
Mother's recovering
from her surgery.
She's not working,
and she's very thin.
I drive her to all her
doctor appointments.
I feel like a good daughter.

I attend gobs of weddings.
I immerse myself in
   The New Yorker
   The Atlantic
   Harper's Magazine.

I'm trying to distill
what makes a story
worth one thousand dollars.

2

The *Writer's Yearbook* magazine
says I should think of myself
    first as a woman,
  then as a writer—
so the inevitable rejections
don't hurl me into
depression.

They say I shouldn't
make my craft my identity.
It's unhealthy.
It will sabotage my
self-esteem.

I'm not sure I can do it,
but I etch the words
into my brain.

3

Hurricane Connie

thrashes us for two days.
I drive to Cambridge
in pouring rain to
look at the devastation.

It exhilarates me,
seeing the power of the sea
and the land that must rebuild.

4

I'm not sure I can do it,
leave home for England.
It's so far away.
What will I do with
the two years I'm there?
Will I let life slip by
only to wake up half dead?
    Life gone?
  All spent with nothing
to show for it?

Can struggle
   in a new, unfamiliar country
and sorrow
   at leaving my home
expand me?

Or will it destroy me?

5

Leaving is what I have to do.
Staying here would
suffocate me.

My wings need practice.

Excitement ripples around me
as I stand on the deck
of the *Queen Elizabeth*,
tangling with fear and expectation
and a tiny sliver of sorrow.

I can't look back.

I leave behind my home,
where everyone knows about
the summer my ocean
nearly swallowed me.
Where my accomplishments
will always live in the
shadow of attempted suicide.

I sail toward a new life.
A new me.

The ocean may rock me to sleep
or overtake me for a moment,
but I know how to master
its waves.

I know how to live.

The sea whispers.
This is my new beginning.
My second chance.

    The sea roars.
    I watch it from the deck,
    my mind ablaze
        alive.

    The sea swells.

    Nothing will
    stop me now.

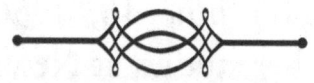

AFTERWORD

Sylvia Plath knew from an early age that she would be remembered. And as one of the most celebrated American poets in the world today—she was. Her poetry and stories have been translated into thirty languages.

Plath is most known for her poems published posthumously, but throughout her life she consistently published her poetry and short stories in magazines and literary journals across the world. She published her first poem when she was eight and had her first short story accepted for publication while in high school.

This book ends with Plath's journey to England—but her life continued its trajectory toward launching Plath to her status as a poet whose work has touched millions of people across generations and countries. On February 25, 1956, a little more than six months after this story ends, Plath met fellow poet and her future husband, Ted Hughes, at a party in Cambridge. They married on June 16, 1956, after which Plath finished her studies at Newnham College, one of two women-only colleges affiliated with the University of Cambridge in England.

When Plath married Hughes, she diminished a little in his shadow—not because he was a better poet but because she *believed* he was a better poet. She focused more of her efforts on sending his work out to be published instead of her own writing. In fact, some believe Hughes would not have been published or discovered if Plath hadn't submitted his work as diligently and consistently as she'd submitted her own before their marriage.

Plath's first book of poetry, *The Colossus*, was published in October 1960, six months after the birth of Plath's first child, Frieda. It was the only book of her poetry published during her lifetime.

A second pregnancy in February 1961 ended in miscarriage. In August of that year, Plath finished *The Bell Jar*, her first novel, before she and Hughes welcomed their second child, Nicholas, in January 1962.

Plath discovered Hughes was having an affair in July 1962. The discovery sent her to her pen, where she wrote scathing poetry about him. In September of that year, they separated. And in October, Plath wrote most of the poems for which she's known today—penning at least twenty-six of her collection *Ariel* during the last months of her life. She drew on her emotional burdens to write her poetry, and her poetry helped her process her emotional burdens. But she did not have the support she needed to navigate the deep waters of depression.

The Bell Jar, Plath's only novel, was published January 14, 1963, under the pseudonym Victoria Lucas. (After she died, it would be rereleased under her real name—and cause quite a scandal because of its biographical narrative.) Less than one month later, Plath died by suicide, on February 11, 1963. She was thirty years old.

Even still, her brilliance lives on.

If you or someone you know is having thoughts of suicide or struggling with suicidal ideation, please reach out for help.

988 Suicide & Crisis Lifeline
988lifeline.org
Call or text 988 or chat at 988lifeline.org.
Free, confidential, and available 24/7/365.

Crisis Text Line
crisistextline.org
Text HOME to 741741 to chat with a trained counselor. Free, confidential, and available 24/7.

The Trevor Project
thetrevorproject.org/crisis-services
Crisis intervention and suicide prevention for LGBTQ+ young people. Free, confidential, and available 24/7.

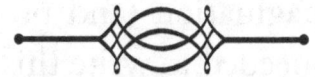

AUTHOR'S NOTE

The first time I read a Sylvia Plath poem, I was in middle school. I immediately searched for everything of hers I could find on the shelves of my local library. This led me to her collected journals and letters and her famous novel, *The Bell Jar*. I was properly obsessed and continued to read every biography published about her into adulthood.

I owe a debt of gratitude to all those biographers as well as the editors of *The Letters of Sylvia Plath* and *The Unabridged Journals of Sylvia Plath*—but the biggest debt I owe is to Heather Clark, who wrote *Red Comet: The Short Life and Blazing Art of Sylvia Plath*. Never before had I read such an exhaustive biography about one of my favorite people. What I loved most was that Clark presented Plath's life and art not through the lens of her suicide, as many others had done, but through the lens of her identity—a complicated, emotional, ambitious woman. It ignited my imagination (and provided valuable information I needed to write this book).

I wanted *Love, Sivvy* to be the same kind of book. Because I connected so much with her letters and journal writings when I was a young adult, I wanted to shine a light on her young adulthood and bring *that* Sylvia to life on the page. I wanted to show Sylvia as her young, vibrant, moody, hopeful self, brimming with promise—because she was.

Sylvia rebelled against the traditional norms of 1950s and '60s womanhood; even her marriage to Ted Hughes was scandalously egalitarian— far more equal than most marriages at that time (Sylvia and Hughes traded off childcare duties so they could both write).

I wanted to capture Sylvia's young adult view about the expectations placed on women. Her journals and some of her poems were a powerful voice for feminism, though she's not one of the voices we typically think about when we consider historical feminist leaders. She was ahead of her time. She knew what she wanted. And she gave everything she had to get there.

These years of her life were when Sylvia began

to realize her potential. When she began to really understand that her dream might be possible. Her moods were up and down, and she made her first suicide attempt in 1953, but she also began learning a little more about how to deal with her moods and depression—though not nearly enough. She had the worries of a teenager and young adult, she enjoyed dating around and keeping her options open, and she was determined not to settle for less than what she wanted.

I suppose one of the many reasons I connected with Sylvia's writing was that she had such strong ambition and conviction that she would accomplish something great in spite of the barriers she faced (money struggles, major depression with suicidal ideation, a world and society that didn't value women). I had strong ambition and conviction that I would accomplish something great in spite of the barriers I faced (money struggles, major depression with suicidal ideation, a world and society that didn't value women). At that time, and even now, women are not always allowed their ambition and conviction that they'll accomplish something great. But we *are* ambitious. We do great things every day. Sylvia gave voice to something so many young women need to hear, even today: that we deserve and are capable of achieving our dreams. That we are not only meant to be wives and mothers or helpers or pretty faces. That we can be ourselves and that is enough.

I've taken liberties as a writer and reimagined conversations between Sylvia and her family, friends, teachers, and dates. I cut much of her dating life (yes! There was more!) from the pages, and I changed some names and moved some things around for the purpose of creating a streamlined narrative—but I believe I've captured the spirit of Sylvia Plath as her young adult self. I hope in these pages I've honored her as a poet, as a woman, and as a trailblazer.

Sylvia knew she would be remembered. She knew she would be great. And she did become great.

And that, to me, means we can, too.

If you want to read more about Sylvia Plath, here are the best places to start:
The Bell Jar
Ariel: The Restored Edition
The Unabridged Journals of Sylvia Plath, edited by Karen V. Kukil

The Letters of Sylvia Plath, Volume 1: 1940–1956, edited by Peter K. Steinberg and Karen V. Kukil

Red Comet: The Short Life and Blazing Art of Sylvia Plath, by Heather Clark

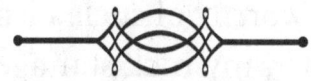

ACKNOWLEDGMENTS

This book was my COVID book. Every author likely has one (just ask them). It took another four years to get it into readable shape and another year to get it into publishing shape, a time period during which many people helped me continue to dive back in with enthusiasm instead of existential dread. Many heartfelt thanks to:

Margaret Raymo, my magnificent editor who fell in love with this manuscript from the beginning and helped me shape it into the book it is today. Thank you for your eagle eye and for making another dream come true.

The team at Little, Brown Books for Young Readers, including Gabrielle Chang, Kathleen Cook, Jen Graham, Stefanie Hoffman, Erica Huang, Savannah Kennelly, Hannah Klein, Roddyna Saint-Paul, and Victoria Stapleton. Thank you for all your tireless efforts getting this book ready to go out into the world and make waves. And to Kimberly Glyder for an arresting, glorious cover worthy of such a legendary poet.

Rena Rossner, my rock star agent. Thank you for always believing in me and my work and helping me make it one hundred times better. Thank you for celebrating every milestone with me. And most of all, thank you for patiently accepting and working toward my giant dreams.

The Zoombies, who never let me give up. I started this book around the same time we started our group, and now it stands as a testament to our connection, community, and endless encouragement. Thank you for always cheering me on.

Mom, for supporting all my obsessions and gifting me with Sylvia Plath's journals when I was a teenager. Look what you made me do. Love you!

J, A, H, B, Z, Ash, my heart, my song, my joy. I love you all so very much and wouldn't change a thing about you or our lives—except maybe I'd keep you small forever.

Ben, the brightest star in my sky. Thank you for always believing in me, for drying my tears, and for reminding me of my purpose. I love our life together, and I'm so grateful we get to live it holding hands. I love you muchly.

Sylvia Plath, for living such a remarkable life and inspiring me as a young writer to find my voice, submit until rejections turned into acceptances, and never back down from what I wanted out of my life. I wish we'd had sixty more years with you.

All the booksellers and librarians who have helped get my books into the hands of young readers everywhere. Thank you for your tireless efforts to protect readers' right to read what they want and need. You are indispensable.

And lastly, you, dear reader. Thank you for picking up this book and reading about the young life of one of the most iconic poets in history. I hope what you've read in these pages gives you the strength and courage to conquer your oceans and live a blazing, remarkable life.

Ben Toalson

R. L. Toalson

is the award-winning author of multiple books for young readers, including *The Unforgettable Leta "Lightning" Laurel*, *The First Magnificent Summer*, *Something Maybe Magnificent*, *The Woods*, and *The Colors of the Rain*. She's a feminist, a runner, and a fierce defender of the freedom to read who enjoys writing poetry and stories of all kinds and reading about the fascinating lives of real people. R. L. invites you to visit her at racheltoalson.com or on Instagram @racheltoalson.

CELEBRATING 100 YEARS OF PUBLISHING

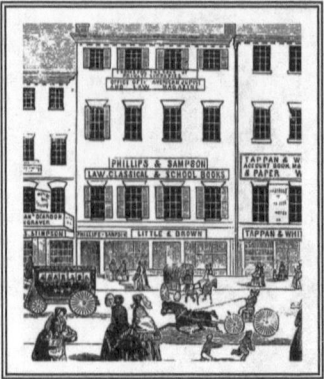

Dear Reader,

You may have noticed the words "Little, Brown and Company" on the title page of this book and wondered what they mean. Well, Charles C. Little and James Brown were the founders of this publishing house, and the "and Company" is all the editors, designers, marketers, publicists, salespeople, and more who help produce each book and bring it to readers like you. Little, Brown was founded in Boston, Massachusetts, in 1837, and some of its early publications included *The Writings of George Washington* and *The Works of Benjamin Franklin*. The catalog grew to feature works by Emily Dickinson and Louisa May Alcott, among many other notable authors. In 1926, recognizing that the literature we read when we are young has a deep and lasting influence and requires expert curation, the company appointed an editor to lead a dedicated children's department.

In 2026, Little, Brown Books for Young Readers celebrates one hundred years of excellence in publishing. Today, we are a division of Hachette Livre, the third-largest publisher in the world, and we are based in New York City. Our staff has grown from a team of two to more than one hundred people. And with the changes in technology, our books are read by more readers, in more ways, and in more countries than ever before. However, one thing has not changed: our commitment to providing a supportive home for all creators and superb stories for all readers. Thank you for being one of them.

Megan Tingley
Megan Tingley
President and Publisher

LITTLE, BROWN AND COMPANY
BOOKS FOR YOUNG READERS

To learn more about Little, Brown's history,
authors, and books, please visit LBYR.com.

www.ingramcontent.com/pod-product-compliance
Lightning Source LLC
LaVergne TN
LVHW031534060526
838200LV00056B/4498